Carl Weber's Kingpins:

Philadelphia

Carl Weber's Kingpins:

Philadelphia

Brittani Williams

www.urbanbooks.net

Urban Books, LLC
97 N18th Street
Wyandanch, NY 11798

Carl Weber's Kingpins: Philadelphia

ISBN 13: 978-1-62286-953-4
ISBN 10: 1-62286-953-2

First Trade Paperback Printing January 2016
Printed in the United States of America

10 9 8 7 6 5 4 3 2 1

Distributed by Kensington Publishing Corp.
Submit orders to:
Customer Service
400 Hahn Road
Westminster, MD 21157-4627
Phone: 1-800-733-3000
Fax: 1-800-659-2436

Carl Weber's Kingpins:

Philadelphia

Brittani Williams

Prologue

Fuckin' Get It Over Wit'

Friday, January 4, 2013, 6:55 p.m.
SCI Rockview, Execution Complex
Bellefonte, Pennsylvania

"I am one of the most hated criminals in four states. I have committed countless acts of violence, which have caused pain to so many. It was never my intention to harm any innocents. It was only my intention to survive the life that was handed to me. While I do not apologize for the things that I had to do, I do apologize for anyone who was caught in the line of fire because of whom they were associated with. I have a date with destiny, and I'm ready to get the party started. For all of those close to me, including the one woman I loved with all of my heart, this isn't the last of me, and I will see you all on the other side."

I never thought that I would be forced to sit and watch someone I loved be murdered right in front of me. But then again, I was never supposed to fall in love to begin with. Thinking back, I couldn't think of a time when my heart and mind were so divided. One part of me was saying, *Kill the bastard,* while the other part was saying, *Please save him.* At exactly 7:00 p.m., five minutes from that moment, the man I vowed to be with for better or for worse would be pronounced dead by way of lethal injection. I sat there stone-faced, trying to hold back the tears that were forcefully making their way to the tips of my tear ducts. I was trained not to let my emotions show, because it could become my downfall. I knew from past experience that there wasn't anything I could do to stop the inevitable and, honestly, I didn't have the urge to try.

As the minutes on the clock counted down, I looked at all of the onlookers, some relatives of those who were victims of his actions, and I felt their pain. I could see it as if it were yesterday, my brother's lifeless body lying in a pool of blood outside of our home and the piercing sound of my mother's screams. One could never truly fathom the pain caused by having a loved one violently ripped from their life. Until you've experienced it first-hand you will never know how it feels. Immediately you question God, and then you're filled with anger and want nothing more but to embark on a trail of revenge. Most people don't have the strength it takes to inflict the same bodily harm as criminals; however, I was cut from a different cloth. This act of revenge was meant to be just the retribution I needed to avenge the death of my brother. Unfortunately, my heart got in the way and was going to be shattered into a million pieces at the same time life left his body.

Most people wondered how I could actually fall in love with a man I hated with every fiber of my being. The truth was, I couldn't truthfully answer that question. There was a part of me that wanted to understand his reasoning. I wanted to know why he did the things that he'd done. Either way, no one would understand the method to the madness that I simply called my life. I was prepared to close this chapter. I was finally going to be able to achieve the justice my family deserved. As a few of the witnesses chanted under their breath, I closed my eyes, playing back the last few years of my life, trying to figure out where things had gone wrong. I'd fought with myself time and time again, with the result always leaving me right where I was sitting.

Just as the time neared two of seven, one of the three telephones on the wall of the anteroom began to ring and a bright red light started to flash over it. The room went silent. You could almost hear a pin drop. The warden walked over to the phone and answered it. The tension in the room immediately grew extremely thick. Everyone began to whisper and look around the room trying to figure out what the holdup was. The warden was doing more listening than he was talking. After the brief conversation, he hung up the phone and looked over to one of the officers near the door. Without any explanation, the curtain was closed and we were told to exit the room. I was in a state of shock. I walked over to an officer to see if he could give me any information about what was happening.

"Hey, what's going on?" I asked as the room emptied.

"The governor has granted a stay of execution," he replied.

My mouth gaped wide open. He could see the confusion written across my face. I knew he'd acquired one of the top lawyers in the city, but I'd never imagined he'd be able to compile enough evidence to stop the execution. Two of the attendees, who I recognized as his associates, filed out of the room, both giving me the evil eye.

Chapter One

I Want You Dead

Desire

There are two types of people in the world: those who run shit and those who get run over. I had experienced many different traumatic events in my lifetime. Most of them were enough to take a person out. If you were weak, you probably wouldn't be able to make it. I have a story to tell, a story about life, death, love, and hate mixed with everything in between. My truth is my truth: either love me or leave me alone. A person isn't born cold-hearted; they are made that way. They are turned when other people force them to be. I was once a girl with goals. I was going somewhere in life until things derailed. Truth was, I should've seen it coming. I should've been more prepared for the bumps in the road.

I wasn't always afraid of guns. The more I think about it, the actual instrument wasn't the source of my fear. I was afraid of the people with the guns more than the guns themselves. I was ten years old the first time I was shot, and to this day I still have nightmares. May 25, 2003 was the day my life changed forever. It was the day that my brother was murdered and I nearly died. At ten years old, all I cared about was Barbie dolls and Baby Alive. I hated boys almost as much as I hated my mother. In my eyes, neither of them meant me any good.

The day had started off the same as any other day. My sister Lala got breakfast ready and my oldest brother Tyrese drove me to school. My mother was always running the streets getting high or somewhere spread eagle, so Tyrese was the primary caretaker for my brother Ali, who was eleven, Lala, who was seventeen, and me. During school I had a weird feeling in my gut. I didn't know what it was or what it meant, but it was something that made me uncomfortable. So much so that I couldn't even eat my lunch. I went through the day, and Tyrese was waiting for me in the same spot at the corner where he always did. I ran over to him, holding my bowling trip permission slip with a huge smile on my face.

"Hey, baby girl," he said, hugging me. "How was school today?"

"Good. We have a trip next week. Mom needs to sign this," I said, excited. I loved school trips because they always gave me an escape from the harsh realities that I lived with daily. Most times, Tyrese forged her signature because she was missing in action.

"I'll sign it for you later. Let's get going, because I have some things to do before dinner," he said, pointing in the direction of his car.

My brother drove a brand new Mercedes at just nineteen. I speculated that his money came from drug dealing, but he'd never admit it to me. I assumed that he thought that was the only way to protect me. It didn't take a rocket scientist to figure out how a teenager without a job could keep our bills paid, food on the table, and name-brand clothing on our backs. I hopped in the passenger seat and immediately turned on the radio.

"What I tell you about that?" He playfully popped me on the back of my hand.

"Please, this is the only time I get to hear Power 99," I said with a sad puppy dog face.

"I know, I know. I'm just joking. Anything to make my baby girl happy." He smiled. "Go ahead and turn it up. Might as well blast it if you really want to hear it!"

I turned the volume up as loud as I could. "Crazy in Love" by Beyoncé was playing. I'd fallen in love with the song as soon as I heard it. I began to sing the words while doing the best seated rendition of her dance moves. Tyrese sat in the driver's seat almost in tears, laughing at me.

I continued to sing as he pulled out of the parking spot and headed toward our house, which was only about ten blocks away. About five blocks into the drive, I noticed a change in his mood. I turned the radio down.

"What's wrong?" I asked with concern.

He was looking into the rearview mirror and fumbling for his cell phone. "Nothing, baby girl. Turn the music back up," he said in a serious tone.

"Something is wrong. Ty, is someone following us?" I asked, turning around in my seat.

"I said nothing is wrong. Now turn the goddamn radio back up," he yelled.

I jumped out of fear. I hated when he yelled. He'd never resorted to hitting me, but I was always afraid that he would. When he was angry, you'd better damn well listen or get the hell out of his way. My hand shook uncontrollably as I turned the volume of the radio back up. I kept my eye on Tyrese as he dialed a number on his Motorola keypad.

"These niggas are on me," he yelled into the receiver. "I'm almost to the crib. Meet me there," he said before putting the phone down and retrieving his gun from his waist.

Tears immediately began to well up in my eyes. I'd never seen a gun up close and personal. Tyrese looked over at me then back into the mirror without saying a word. Normally when I cried, he'd go out of his way to console me. At that moment, my tears didn't seem to evoke any emotion from him. It was almost as if his soul had already left his body.

He sped down through the streets and onto our block before turning into the driveway. He slammed on the brakes and cocked his gun before opening the door and getting out. A black Cadillac had stopped behind us, and within seconds I heard gunshots. I tried to duck down in my chair, but the seat belt had a tight grip around my torso. Tyrese was still standing, shooting in the direction of the black car. I was screaming as glass shattered and bullets flew past me. I could hear the children on the block screaming and scattering.

I finally got the seat belt loose, and just as I opened the door, I heard Tyrese yell in agony. I turned, and he was leaned up against the open driver's side door with blood pouring from multiple gunshot wounds. I climbed over the seat and out on top of him. Trying to shield him, I was struck with a burning pain before my body went numb. I stared my brother in the eye as he gasped for air. The screeching of tires was heard a second later, followed by my mother's screams.

"No, not my baby," she screamed.

She pulled me off of Tyrese and laid me on the ground. The neighbors ran over, all frantic. My mom was cradling Tyrese in her arms as I lay still, with my sister holding her hand over the exit wound in my chest. I couldn't say that I was surprised by my mother's reaction, since I knew for a long time she didn't give a shit about me. Even though I didn't expect her to care, I wished that she had. I wished that she'd cared enough about me not to lay me to the side like a piece of garbage. I know that a situation like this would be tough for any mother, but it was clear which child was important to her. I couldn't feel anything, and everything was becoming a blur.

"Come on, baby, keep your eyes open!" she screamed, shaking Tyrese's head. She was racked with sobs as he was slowly dying in her arms.

Soon I began to feel pain again, and I screamed so loudly the entire group, which had gathered around us, got completely quiet. My mother still stayed holding his limp body while I lay in agony with my sister's hands pressed against my chest. Not once did my mother look to see if I was okay. After a few more seconds, everything went black.

The next thing that I remember was waking up a week and one day later. The first person I saw was my sister Lala.

"Hey, baby girl. How are you feeling?" she asked, getting up from the chair and walking over to the side of the bed. My throat was sore and my chest hurt like hell.

"Where's Ty? Is he okay?" I asked. I didn't care about my injuries. I just wanted to know that he was still alive.

She immediately began to cry and grabbed a hold of my hand.

"No," I screamed through the piercing pain in my throat.

"I'm sorry, D, but he didn't make it. We buried him yesterday."

I began to scream while trying to pull the leads from the heart monitor off of my chest. I wanted to get out of there. At that moment, the closest thing to me was gone. He'd always been more like a father to me than a brother. I ripped the IV out of my arm and blood squirted all over the white bed sheets. Lala tried to calm me as two nurses ran into the room. I was fighting them with everything I had, even causing one of their noses to bleed. I needed to see him. I couldn't wrap my mind around the idea of him being dead. Soon the room was filled with hospital staff trying to calm me down. Eventually I was held down by three staff members and given a needle in my shoulder that immediately made me sleepy.

When I woke up my hands and feet were tied to the bed. Lala was standing over at the window looking outside. I began to tug at the restraints hoping I could get free. She came over to the bed when she realized that I was awake.

"D, you have to calm down. You don't want them to take you away. I need you to pull yourself together. Ty wouldn't want you to fall apart. He loved you too much," she said, placing her hands on both sides of my cheeks and looking me in the eye.

"I'd rather die with him. I can't live without him, Lala, I just can't." Tears were rolling down my cheeks and onto her hands.

"You don't have a choice. We don't have a choice. We have to be strong and make him proud."

"I didn't get a chance to say bye. I tried to save him. I took a bullet in the back for him," I cried.

My body was aching and not from the injury. My heart hurt. My soul was bleeding. The bullet that I thought I stopped went through me and into his heart, killing him. I began to blame myself, thinking if I'd stayed put maybe he would've survived. So many thoughts ran through my mind, and depression was inevitable. To make matters even worse, my mother never visited me. Lala claimed she was too distraught, but somehow, I believed that she blamed me just as much as I blamed myself. Tyrese was the glue that held us all together, and without him things would never be the same.

I was discharged two days later and ended up at my grandmother's house where I remained until I finished school. My mother couldn't look at me without thinking of him. She'd lost the house and car, and her drug addiction grew worse by the day. Thankfully, my grandmother was there to push me along each time I thought about quitting. There wasn't anyone who loved him more than I did, and I believed that she mourned the loss of the things that he provided more than the loss of her child. That day, she lost two children, because I never called her mother again.

I carried around a photo of Tyrese everywhere I went. In the photo he had his arms wrapped around me, and I had the biggest smile on my face. Everything that I did was for him, and I vowed to get revenge on anyone who had something to do with his death. I didn't care who I had to harm in the process. I wanted them all to pay, and death was more fulfilling than any prison stint.

Chapter Two

Son of a Savior . . . or Not

Dontay

Summer, 1988

You know the saying, "You eat shit, you order shit"? Well, that's one of the realest quotes ever spoken. I didn't know who originated the line, but it was one that I'd spit on countless occasions. Where I was from, you only acquired shit you worked to get. Whether it's standing on the corner, working in the trap, robbing niggas, whatever your specialty, you put in many hours of hard-ass labor. The way I interpreted the quote: if you work hard, you get results. If you're a lazy muthafucker who thinks shit should be handed to you on a platter, then keep your ass in the projects. One thing about me was I was a realist and ain't no beating around the bush over here. I never gave a fuck what anyone thought about me. Growing up I was forced to be a man much sooner than I should've been. I was my mother's only child, but my father, he had multiple children by multiple women. Hell, I didn't even know all of them. For all I knew, I could've been fucking my own sister thanks to him. Clearly, I wasn't the son of a preacher man, but I was damn sure the son of a savior. That may sound strange, but the way my mother told it, he took her from a life of poverty and showered her with nothing but the best. By the time I was five, they were no longer together, but my father made sure we always had and never wanted for anything. That was, until he got married. I was ten years old when I realized shit had changed.

It was the summer of 1988, and it was hotter than a muthafucker. I woke up sweating half to damn death in a house that was pitch-black. I got out of bed and rubbed my eyes, trying to maneuver my way through the house without falling and breaking my neck. Once I made it to the hall I could hear my mother's voice. She was on the phone yelling.

"What do you mean you can't pay the bills anymore, Jimmy? Your son lives here," she yelled. "So you're gonna let that bitch dictate how you take care of your responsibilities?"

I made my way to the top of the stairs to finish eavesdropping. This was the first time I'd ever heard my parents have an argument.

"It's ninety-five degrees outside, Jimmy. We are in here in the dark with no air. You could've at least given me a warning," she yelled with her voice cracking. I could tell from where I stood that she was trying hard to fight back tears.

"You know what, Jimmy? Fuck you and that bitch. I hope both of you go straight to hell with gasoline drawers on," she yelled before slamming the phone down.

A few seconds later I heard the sound of her lighter followed by the burning of her Newport cigarette. I didn't want her to know that I'd heard her conversation so I tried to tiptoe back to my room. I hadn't noticed my skateboard in the middle of the floor, and stubbed my toe.

"Ouch," I said aloud as I bent down to move the skateboard out of the way.

"Dontay?" my mother hollered up the stairs.

"Yes, Mom," I replied.

"Come downstairs so I can talk to you for a minute."

"Okay," I said as I made my way back toward the stairs. I crept down the stairs already having it in my head that I would act clueless of what I'd heard. She was sitting on the sofa near the door. I walked over and sat down next to her. "What's wrong with the electricity, Mom? It's hot in here."

"I know, baby. I'll have to wait until they open up and go over to take care of the bill. I honestly forgot that it was due, but I'll take care of it. You can go around your grandmom's if it's too hot in here for you."

"No, it's okay," I replied. I knew that she hadn't forgotten about the bill. I didn't want her to feel even worse that she already did by running to my grandmom.

"Why don't you go take a cold shower. That should help you cool off. It'll only be a couple of hours before they open," she said.

"Okay," I said as I got up and went back upstairs.

The light was starting to peek in through the blinds. This was the first time that we'd ever experienced any type of hardship. I hated to see my mother upset. At ten, there wasn't much that I could do to fix the problem. I thought that maybe if I went and talked to my father myself, he would have a little sympathy and give us the bill money.

After my mom left, I got dressed, put on my backpack, and went out to walk to my father's house. I didn't tell my mom about my intentions because I knew that she would never approve. It took me an hour and a half to make it to his home by foot. I was hot and exhausted. I didn't see my father's Mercedes sitting in the driveway. As a matter of fact, there was a FOR SALE sign sticking out of the grass. I became enraged as I thought about the fact that he'd up and leave. I walked behind the rosebush that sat in front of one of the windows and tried to look inside. All of the furniture was gone. Nothing was visible except the newly polished cherry-wood floors. I walked around to the rear of the house and that was empty as well. The patio door appeared to be cracked open so I went over and tugged it open. I walked inside slowly.

"Hello. Is anybody home?" I said. The last thing I needed was someone coming out and shooting my ass. Satisfied that I was alone I walked in every room and each room was empty. I was on my way out of the back door when something came over me. I wanted him to pay. The only thing that I could think of doing at the time was damaging his home and putting a halt to his sale. I went in my backpack and pulled out my pencil case. Inside were crayons, markers, paint, you name it. I took every color of every medium I had and marked up the freshly painted white walls. In every room I wrote FUCK YOU and GO TO HELL. My handwriting was terrible, but you could understand what I was saying loud and clear. I threw colored paint all over the floors and countertops in the kitchen. The tile in the bathroom was covered with a nice shade of red. I was furious before I even truly understood what fury felt like.

Once I was satisfied with the damage I picked up my backpack and left the same way that I'd come in. This time, instead of walking, I ran as fast as I could. I ran about twenty blocks before I stopped running. I bent over breathing heavily. After getting a second wind, I continued home. Once I got there my mother was on the steps with an angry face. She got up once she noticed me.

"Where the hell have you been, Dontay? Why would you leave the house without telling me where you were going? And what the hell happened to your clothes? Why are you covered with paint?" she asked without stopping to take a breath in between questions.

"I'm sorry, Mom. I went to the playground with my friends and lost track of time," I lied.

"Don't you ever do that shit again. Do you understand me?"

"Yes, Mom, I understand."

"Now go in the house and get cleaned up. I'll fix you lunch in a few minutes."

I went inside and immediately felt the cool air. The electricity was back on. At least I could sleep comfortably. I went and took off my soiled clothes and took my second shower of the day. Just as I was getting out I heard a commotion downstairs followed by loud screams. I hurried and put on my boxers and opened the door. As I ran to the stairs, I saw my father and mother in the living room, arguing.

"I know it was you, Olivia. You really came and threw paint all over my fucking house like a goddamn child?" he yelled.

"I didn't come to your house. I was at the electric company trying to get my service cut back on since you decided to cut us off."

"No one else but you would do that shit. I wasn't born yesterday. That shit won't make me come back to you and it damn sure won't make me give you no fucking money. You have to be the most vindictive bitch I know."

"Bitch? Really, Jimmy? Now I'm a bitch 'cause you got your little wife now. Fuck you! Get the fuck out of my house," she yelled pushing him.

Immediately he pushed her back making her fall to the ground. I ran down the stairs as fast as I could to come to her aid. He was walking over to her with his fists balled up.

"Stop it! Don't hit her," I yelled standing in between them.

"Stay out of grown folks' business, boy. Get out the way," he yelled pushing me aside.

"Stop. It wasn't her. It was me. I did it, okay? I damaged the house," I said with tears forming.

He stood there silent before swiftly hitting me with a backhand across the face that lifted me up off the ground. I landed on top of my mother.

"Just leave, okay? Just go. I'll never ask you for anything again. Just leave us alone," my mother cried as she cradled me in her arms. Her tears were running down her cheeks and landing on my face.

"Fuck this and fuck y'all," he said before turning and walking out of the door.

"It's okay, baby. We'll be fine. We'll be just fine."

Chapter Three

Motherless

Desire

"Lala, I'm gonna walk to school today. You don't have to drive me," I said as I ran down the stairs and grabbed my school bag off the hook near the front door.

"Why not?" she asked with one hand on her right hip.

"Because I just want to walk."

"You better not be up to nothing. Did you say bye to Mom?"

"For what? She never says bye to me," I said, rolling my eyes.

"Stop it, D. You know she's depressed."

"Shit, so am I! I gotta go or I'm gonna be late." I hurried out of the door before she could reply.

I wasn't in the mood to argue with her about that shell of a woman. Honestly, it wasn't worth my breath. I'd made it through the past six years without her as a mother, so there wasn't any need to fake it now. Neither of us was interested in the other's well-being, and that was one thing she'd passed on to me that I could actually appreciate. I hurried around the block and quickly made it to my girl Octavia's house. She was standing on the steps, waiting for me.

"About time," she said, rolling her neck.

"Sorry. I was trying to make sure my outfit was together."

"I hope that's not what you're wearing."

"Hell, no. It's under here. Let me go fix my makeup then we can go."

"Girl, you're lucky my mom already left for work. We have to hurry before my dad comes back."

"Okay. I only need ten minutes." I ran inside and up the stairs to her bedroom and quickly took off the long dress the concealed the miniskirt and cropped top I had on underneath. In record time I was dressed to impress. I checked to make sure I looked perfect. We were on our way over to the Hangout, a local strip club and lounge where all the dope boys hung out. We were going over to my girl Shany's house until it opened at noon since her parents both worked the day shift. That would give us enough time to sneak a few drinks out of her daddy's cabinet to get nice and tipsy.

"Hurry up!" Octavia yelled.

"Okay, okay," I said as I gathered my things and ran down the stairs. "I'm ready, damn."

"Yeah, you'll really be screaming damn if my dad comes in and catches us."

"All right, let's go."

We walked the five blocks to Shany's house and went in through the yard like we always did when we cut school. There were too many nosy-ass old people on her block, and they would surely run and tell her mom we were there.

"About time y'all got here," she said as we entered the shed kitchen.

"Where the drinks at?" I said with a big-ass smile and a giggle. I was ready to get the party started.

"Right here. What you want? I got vodka, gin, rum. My daddy got all the good shit in here," Shany said, walking over to the liquor cabinet.

"Give me the rum," Octavia said.

"Yeah, me too. Last time that gin fucked up my stomach," I said.

She poured us all a glass. We sat at the table sipping and talking. I'd been eyeing this one guy for the past month. He was much older than me so I knew he wouldn't be interested in me unless I could convince him that I was older than I really was.

"I'm hoping today is the day," I said.

"The day for what?" Octavia said setting her glass down on the table.

"That I get his attention."

"And what do you plan to do when you do? Huh? Little Miss Virgin." Shany burst out laughing.

"I haven't thought that far yet," I replied.

"Well, you know those niggas ain't paying no attention to someone who ain't giving up the pussy," Shany said.

"Who said that I wouldn't give it up? Just because I'm a virgin now doesn't mean I'll be one forever."

Honestly, I was ready to have sex, but I didn't want them to know that. I was tired of being the butt of their jokes. I knew that I would need more than brains to snag a dope boy, but I'd do whatever it took to make sure I was on one of their arms. I wanted a man who was just like Tyrese: smart, street smart, fine as hell with tons of money. I refused to settle for anything less than the boss, because that's what Tyrese was. Yeah, being with a man like that had a lot of risks, but it was worth it to me.

"So what time are we going to head over?" I asked, changing the subject. Anything to take the attention off of me.

"I guess we can leave out around twelve unless y'all have somewhere else you want to go on the way," Shany said.

"No, twelve is cool," Octavia replied.

We sat and talked for the next few hours before we were on our way. We didn't need fake IDs to get in since Shany was sleeping with the bouncer at the door. Octavia and I made our way inside while Shany stayed at the door chatting with her boo. There were a few people scattered around the place. We only came here on Fridays, because that was the day the real bosses made an appearance.

"You wanna get a drink?" Octavia asked.

"If I drink anything else I'll probably vomit. I'm good."

"Well, shit, I need one. Walk me to the bar," she said, grabbing me by the arm, and dragging me along to the bar.

She sat down on the stool as I stood next to her watching the door. I was waiting for him to appear: Dontay, my dream man. He was running shit on this side of town. From what I heard, he inherited the business from his brother, but I wasn't sure how much of that was the truth. You know how the streets are: you can't believe everything you hear.

"Girl, stop looking desperate. Sit your ass down. If he's coming you'll know when he arrives," she said, pulling me over to the stool.

"I'm not looking desperate. I just like to watch my surroundings," I replied as I slid onto the stool.

"Whatever. Here, I got you a drink." She slid me a cup.

I was daydreaming so hard that I hadn't even heard her order it. "I said I didn't want anything else to drink."

"When have I ever listened to you?"

"Never."

"Exactly. Now take a damn sip and relax."

I tried my best to relax. I was bobbing my head to the music and enjoying myself.

"Yo, send three bottles over to Dontay," a male voice screamed over the music to the bartender.

I almost spit my drink out when I heard his name. I slowly turned my chair around as the man made his way over to the back. There he sat, looking like he'd stepped off the pages of a *GQ* magazine.

"He's here," I said to Shany and Octavia as they were engrossed in a conversation about their men.

"I know, he's been here. I saw him when he came in," Shany replied.

"Well, why the hell didn't you say anything?"

"Because I knew you'd get all hype and play yourself. Just chill. If it's meant to be, he'll notice you."

I wanted to pout like a five-year-old, but I didn't. I just turned back around and began to think about what I would say if I ever got the chance to have a conversation with him. An hour later, I still hadn't gotten so much as a glance from him. I was feeling defeated. I was ready to go.

"What time are y'all planning to leave? I'm over this," I said.

"We can leave now if you want. It's almost two-thirty anyhow. That'll give me enough time to get home before three," Shany said.

"Yeah, I'm ready," I said.

"Cool, let's go," Octavia said.

We made our way to the door. As Shany stood and kissed her man Lou good-bye, Octavia and I stood to the side, waiting. Just then, Dontay and some big-ass nigga walked out of the club. He was huge. I figured it was his security or something. I froze while trying not to stare too hard. For a second we made eye contact. He smiled, licked his sexy lips, and chuckled before walking over to an all-black Ford Expedition across the street. He hopped in the passenger seat and just as they drove off he smiled at me once more. I almost jumped out of my miniskirt I was so excited.

"He smiled at me, did you see it?" I said with the biggest grin on my face.

"Really, D? He smiled? You are whipped and you haven't even gotten any yet," Octavia said as she laughed.

I didn't even respond. Even if she didn't see it as a big deal, I did. A smile was more than I'd ever gotten from him. At that moment, I was on cloud nine, and I knew that things could only get better from there.

Chapter Four

Life's a Bitch

Alisha

I was twelve when it happened. The day the Johnson boys ripped my young pussy to shreds. I was on my way back home from the store and was distracted by the kids playing in the fire hydrant. I'd just gotten my hair done so I was praying that none of the boys would pick me up and throw me into the water. My mom had sent me to pick up a few things for dinner. We were always struggling financially and since she sold most of her food stamps for drugs we often survived off of hot dogs, baked beans, and anything else sold in the corner Papi store.

I was walking at a fast pace but steadily keeping my eye on the kids at play. After a few steps, I tripped and fell flat on my face, dropping the bags that I carried. The cans of baked beans rolled out of the bag and into the street. I felt a stinging in my bottom lip and once I licked it, I tasted blood. I started to get up off the ground and was immediately pulled into the lot near the corner. I tried to scream but my mouth was covered by a pair of strong hands. I was kicking and grabbing at the arms that were tightly wrapped around my body preventing me from getting loose. I was pulled through an open door at the end of the lot, which led into the basement of an abandoned house. Once inside I was thrown onto a filthy mattress. The stench of piss flowed up through my nostrils causing me to gag and almost vomit. I heard laughing as I turned around attempting to get up off the mattress.

"Lay your ass back down, bitch," Jesse Johnson said, shoving me back onto the mattress.

"Please don't hurt me," I cried. I was scared shitless.

"What you wanna do with her, Rick?" Jesse asked his older brother.

The Johnson boys were notorious in the neighborhood for starting shit. They'd also been known for forcing themselves on the young females around the way. Their father was a sergeant for the police department; therefore, they always got off scot-free. Jesse was fifteen and Rick was seventeen. Both of them were large for teenagers. Rick was all muscle while Jesse was fat as fuck. I couldn't stand either of them, and I tried my best to steer clear of them.

"I wanna fuck that young pussy that's what I want to do. Matter of fact I want to taste it first. Pull her panties off. Yo, Trey, come help him!" Rick hollered out to one of their cousins, Trey, who was all of six feet tall and two hundred pounds.

I continued to cry and plead with them. Jesse and Trey came over and began tugging at my shorts and then my panties. I kicked and screamed until Jesse hit me over the head causing me to get a bit dizzy.

"Please stop. I'm a virgin," I cried.

"Shit, virgin pussy is the best pussy. Hurry up," Rick yelled.

I was sobbing so hard my entire body began to shiver.

"Grab that rope and tie her hands up," Rick instructed.

The two teens grabbed my arms and tied them tightly behind my back. I was naked from the waist down.

"Hold her legs. Spread that pussy open. Umm you see that shit? It's fat, too, damn," Rick said, rubbing on his dick through his jeans. He got down on his knees as the two boys spread my legs apart as wide as they could. My young pussy was staring him in the face. I wasn't sure what he was about to do, but I knew it couldn't be good. The next thing I felt was his tongue on the lips and then his fingers spreading them apart. I jumped and continued to cry. I closed my eyes and began to say a silent prayer. He licked, sucked, and slurped on my pussy for the next ten minutes as tears fell freely from my eyes.

"Please stop," I begged. He stopped but only to stuff a dirty-ass rag off the floor into my mouth.

"Shut your ass up and enjoy it. Most bitches love their pussy ate," Rick yelled as both Jesse and Trey giggled.

Rick got back on his knees and assumed the position. He sat up and unzipped his pants releasing his dick from his boxers. Both Trey and Jesse turned away briefly while his dick was in their view.

"Open her up some more for me," he instructed. Then he moved close to me and tugged at my shirt. "Let me see those titties."

My breasts were now exposed as he roughly rubbed on them. Without warning, he shoved his dick inside of my tunnel, and I screamed in agony. The sound was muffled by the rag in my mouth, but I was sure it could still be heard a block away. I'd never felt pain so excruciating.

"Damn, bitch, this pussy is tight!" he moaned as he continued to force his dick inside of me as deep as he could get it. For the next twenty minutes or so he fucked me like there was no tomorrow. The entire time I kept my eyes squinted tightly. Then suddenly his body began to shake. "Aww shit I'm cumming, goddamn, bitch," he said before stopping and removing his dick from inside of me. I could feel the wetness and fluids he'd deposited running out of me. I was praying that they'd be done, but they weren't.

"My turn," Jesse's fat ass yelled.

Rick came around and grabbed my leg so that Jesse could get free. Then for another half hour Jesse fucked me as well. I found myself wishing I would just die. I couldn't think of anything worse happening and believed that death had to be better. Once Jesse was done it was Trey's turn.

"That pussy is all loose now. Turn her over so I can get in that ass," he said.

Rick and Jesse turned me over. I could hear Trey loosening his belt and heard his pants drop down. Then I heard him spit a few times and a weird sound. Then he spread my ass cheeks open and spit in between them before rubbing his hands up and down my ass crack. Then he forced his dick inside my ass. I felt it tearing. My body was tensing up even more. The pain was so unbearable that I passed out.

When I woke up I was lying on the mattress still naked and in pain. My hands were free, but I couldn't find my clothes anywhere. At that point my goal was to get out of there and get home as fast as I could. I ran up the steps and out of the lot toward the street ass naked. People pointed, laughed, and some gasped as my naked body flew down the block. There was blood and fluid running in between my thighs. When I finally made it up the steps and into the house, I fell to the floor in the foyer.

"Mom. Somebody help me," I yelled.

My mother appeared with a cigarette in her hand. "What the fuck is going on here?"

"Ma, I was attacked. The Johnson boys raped me," I cried. I wanted her to make me feel better just as a mother should when her child is hurting, but instead she became angry.

"See, that's your fucking fault! You see what being cute does for you? Huh? You so fast to walk out here in tight-ass clothes and shit. That's what the fuck you get. Carry your ass upstairs and take a bath. Bet you'll listen to me now." She took a puff of her cigarette.

"Mom, I'm bleeding. I need to go to a doctor," I begged.

"You don't need no doctor. They just busted your cherry, that's all. Get upstairs and take a bath, and keep your ass in that room and think about what you've caused. This shit is your fault, so you can't blame nobody but yourself for this shit!" she yelled before turning and walking back toward the kitchen.

I peeled myself from the floor and began walking up the steps when she appeared again.

"Where the fuck is the food I told you to get?"

"It rolled out in the street when they grabbed me," I cried. She was actually more concerned about fucking baked beans than her own child.

"When you're dressed, carry your ass out there and find my shit and bring it back." She turned around and walked back into the kitchen.

Her lack of empathy, or sympathy for that matter, was something that I had grown used to. She wasn't the type of mother who would hug and kiss us good-bye. Her coldness was one of the reasons that I grew up cold. We weren't raised in a loving environment so we never learned how to properly show love. I was always jealous of my friends and the relationships that they had with their parents. Deep down, I always wished that I could trade places with them, but that wish would never be granted no matter how much I prayed for it.

I walked up to the bathroom and slammed the door. I sat in the tub and soaked for a few minutes. I was crying so loud my siblings were at the door knocking to see if

I was okay. I didn't respond. I couldn't let them know what'd just happened to me. I was embarrassed. Maybe she was right. Maybe it was my fault. Maybe if I'd listened better none of this would've occurred.

My bath was cut short when she entered the bathroom and threw some clothes at me. I got out of the tub and put on the clothes before going to see if I could find the food I'd lost. Luckily the items had rolled under a car and were still there. I looked up thanking God, because I was afraid of the whipping I was sure to get had I not found them. I picked them up and ran back home.

Chapter Five

The Aftermath

Alisha

Getting shot twice in the chest can do one of two things: kill you or wake you the fuck up! I never expected that my life would end up in such disarray, but you can chalk that up to my naiveté. I was that bitch who thought I could do whatever I wanted, whenever I wanted, and get away with it. The funny thing about life is that you can never take shit back, and karma is the baddest bitch on earth.

Thinking back, I probably wouldn't have done things any differently, because I was just doing what I was taught to do. I had a mother who didn't give a shit about us. She was more concerned about the increase of her monthly food stamps that came with bearing an additional child. Being the eldest child, I didn't have a choice: either do what she said or get the fuck out.

My mother was one who knew how to use her body to get anything she needed. Our door had so much traffic the shit was practically hanging off the hinges. The aroma of our apartment matched the scent of her stank pussy and the sweaty balls of the trifling niggas she fucked on a regular basis. It was embedded in our clothing like people who have a million roaches. It was embarrassing to say the least. I would hand-wash my clothes, and hang them out on the line hoping to get rid of the funk, but it never worked, regardless of the amount of Tide or bleach I used. Needless to say, my childhood was something that I'd give my last dime to wipe completely out of my mental bank.

I never understood how a man could be so desperate for pussy that he'd pay for it. I finally figured it out when my body began to develop, and boys would chase me like their last meal. I was blessed with one of the softest and roundest asses that you'd ever see without any surgical enhancements. At the age of sixteen I was blessed with the measurements 32DD-25-42. My titties stood at attention, too, without the need for a bra. I hated bras so I barely wore them. If I did, it was to conceal my hard nipples during school hours. On top of that I had a pretty face and a fat pussy. I was the shit in every sense of the word. Once I realized that I was blessed with the tools to keep my pockets fat, I never wanted for anything. I remember my mother saying, "If you're gonna spread your legs and let them taste your pussy, you better make sure you don't leave with anything less than a hundred dollars in your pocket!"

Back then I thought she was trying to tell me to be a prostitute, but she was just teaching me the game. That's about the only good thing that I gained from having her as a mother. Other than that, I could've done a better damn job of raising my siblings than she was even capable of. She died from a cocaine overdose when I was seventeen. Burying her was the best present I'd ever received to this day.

That may sound fucked up, but anybody who thought that I deserved the shit that happened to me could die slow as far as I was concerned. I didn't kill anyone, not with my own hands, so in my book I didn't deserve to be killed.

I woke up in the hospital feeling like I had been beaten with a bag full of bricks. Every inch of my body hurt, and my chest felt like a 500-pound bitch had sat on it. There weren't any cards, flowers, or balloons in my room and not one visitor, except my baby sister, Hope. Most people would've preferred to see me in a casket, but God always has a plan.

Hope was asleep in the recliner over near the window covered up with a white hospital blanket. She was my ride or die bitch, and I knew the only thing that could've kept her away from my bedside was her own death. I cleared my sore-ass throat before I called out her name to wake her up.

"Hope, wake up," I yelled at the loudest volume that I could force.

She jumped up like I had scared the shit out of her. I began to laugh as if I'd just heard the funniest joke.

"That shit ain't funny, Alisha! Damn, you know I hate when you do that shit. You lucky you all fucked up right now 'cause I'd pop you one." She laughed.

"I'm glad to see nothing's changed." I laughed. She'd always been feisty.

"What did you think, you being shot would change how I talk to you? Shit, I'm still the same firecracker baby sister you've always had ready to put a bitch in their place. I can't just kick your ass right now, that's all." She continued to laugh while walking over to the side of the bed, and sitting down.

"Did they catch that nigga?" I asked. I was anxious to find out the fate of Dontay.

"Naw, but he'll get his. I have something in the works for his ass."

"Something like what? He's dangerous, Chas. I don't need you to defend my honor. The cops will catch him and deal with it."

"Fuck the cops, Alisha. They don't give a fuck about you. You really think you are their first priority? You can wait on that shit if you want, but I'm not. Fuck that! You're the only family I have, and I almost lost you. Somebody has to pay for that shit."

She got up from the bed, and paced the floor. I'd never seen her so angry. I had always been the one to step up, and take care of shit when things got out of control. If this had been a few years ago, I would've been gearing up to go to war, but things were different now. I was given another chance at life, and I didn't want to waste it.

"Chas, he shot me so I'm pissed, but look at all of the shit that I've done. It could've been worse. I could be dead. I need you."

"I'm sorry, but I'm not going to just sit around and watch this muthafucker walk around like he didn't do shit. He deserves to suffer. I'm not going to do anything to get myself killed, I promise."

"Well, at least wait until I'm back on my feet so that I can help you," I pleaded. I was hoping that once I was better I could talk her out of whatever warped idea she had in her mind.

"This isn't up for discussion. Shit is already in motion so I need you to focus on getting better. That's all you need to worry about right now. I got this."

I looked at her and saw so much of myself. If there was one thing in the world that I regretted, it was passing on the fucked-up mentality that I once had. I knew what I wanted and never cared what I did or who I had to hurt to get there. The game had taken so much from us. Hell, both of my brothers were murdered.

She continued to talk, but I couldn't hear her. I had drifted back in time thinking about all of the mistakes that I'd made, and trying to figure out what I could do to change her fate. I didn't want her to end up like me. I would die trying to make shit right. I knew that I'd created a monster, but it was time for this shit to stop, point blank period.

Chapter Six

Trouble

Dontay

For the next few years, things were tough. I could remember my mother selling all of her jewelry and furs to pay the bills. Eventually, she went and got a job at the Shop-N-Bag supermarket. By the time I was fifteen, I was determined to make enough money to help her out. I didn't know any other way to get money legally at that age so the streets were my outlet. That's where my best friend Rick came in.

Rick was a big-ass nigga for his age. Shit, he was big for any damn age to be honest. At fifteen, he stood six foot two and weighed well over 200 pounds. He wasn't a bully like most big kids were, but everyone knew not to fuck with him. He was known to knock niggas on their ass for testing him. He was strong as hell, too. I'd see him knock countless niggas out cold. So because of his size and strength, he was given the nickname Horse. His older brother, Nate, was a pretty well-known drug dealer. At the time, he was only nineteen, but already had five years in the game. Horse was always talking about working for his brother, and after I grew tired of waiting I finally approached the subject seriously.

School had just let out and, as usual, Horse and me walked the long way through the neighborhood. We would shoot the breeze and holler at the chicks we'd pass along the way. We'd also always stop in the Papi store on the corner to grab a few snacks. We'd always walk through the block where Nate and his crew hung out so, before we got there, I wanted to ask Horse to talk to Nate.

"Let me ask you something, Horse," I said as we stopped at the red light.

"What's up?" he asked, snacking on the barbecue chips he held in his hands.

"You're always talking about getting down with Nate and his crew. I wanted to know if I could get down too."

"Huh? Not Mr. College Bound." He laughed.

"I'm being serious right now. I'm tired of watching my mom struggling and shit. I want to see her laidback with her feet up on some island. Not standing for ten hours at a damn supermarket for chump change."

"You really serious, bro?" he asked as he stopped walking.

"Dead serious, man. I really need this. I'll start from the bottom. Whatever I need to do to prove myself."

"All right, man, let's go see if he's on the block. I'll holler at him for you."

"Thanks, man," I said as I gave him a quick handshake and hug.

We walked around York Street to find Nate and a few of his boys sitting on the corner steps.

"What's up, niggas," Horse said, raising his hands up in the air. "Yo, Nate, I need to holler at you for a second."

"A'ight," Nate said as he and Horse walked around the corner just out of view.

I stood there with Nasir, Jungle, and Lou as they passed around a tightly rolled blunt. "You want some, li'l nigga?" Jungle asked.

"Naw, I'm good," I replied. I stood listening to their conversation for the next five minutes until Horse called me to the corner.

"Yo, Dontay, come here for a minute," Horse said, waving his hands.

I walked around the corner. Nate was posted up against the pay phone sipping on a Colt 45 with a lit cigarette in his left hand. "So Horse tells me you want to work for me," he said before puffing his cigarette and blowing out smoke.

"Yeah, man. I really need to get on. Shit is rough over at the crib. I'm tired of watching my mom struggle."

"What's up wit' that nigga Jimmy Black? Ain't that yo' daddy?"

"Man, fuck that nigga. That's my sperm donor. He don't deserve to be called Daddy," I said through clenched teeth. Just the mention of him made my blood boil.

"All right, li'l nigga, don't bite my head off. I don't like that muthafucker anyway. What's good with the security at y'all school? Do they be watching y'all?"

"Nah, they don't really fuck with us like that. They pretty chill in there."

"All right. Well, I'ma give you a shot because you're his right-hand man, but don't fuck me over. I won't have a problem bussin' a cap in your ass," he said as he pointed to the gun on his waist.

"Horse is like my brother, man. I would never do you like that. I really need this shit, man. I appreciate you even thinking about giving me a chance."

"I'm gonna set y'all up with some small bags of weed. I want y'all to take that shit to school and move it. Depending on how well y'all do with that, I'll decide if I want to give y'all some real work," he said.

"Thanks a lot, man. I really appreciate it," I said.

"Come by the crib in the morning and I'll give y'all the work, a'ight?"

"Thanks, bro. See you later," Horse said.

After shaking our hands Nate walked away and returned to his group of friends. We began to walk through the park.

"Man, I can't wait to get this shit started," I said, excited.

"Nigga, calm down. Don't go broadcasting the shit and get yourself locked up. You gotta be discreet about that shit."

"I know, I know, man. I'm just looking forward to being straight."

"Everything is gonna be all good. We just gotta move this work. If Nate is impressed he'll really put us on. This is just a test."

"I already have a game plan in my head. I know all the weed heads, and all the chicks who love to get high. I'm planning on getting rid of all that shit tomorrow. Watch what I tell you," I said with confidence.

I was a firm believer that I could do anything that I put my mind to. I was going to work harder than I ever had before. After making it to the corner of my block, we parted ways with a handshake and hug.

"See you tomorrow, my nigga," Horse said.

"You most certainly will," I said with a huge smile on my face.

I walked down to the house with my mind going a mile a minute. As soon as I got home, I pulled out one of my notebooks, grabbed a pen, and sat down on my bed. Inside, I made a list of all of the people I knew for sure would be customers. On the opposite page, I wrote down all of the "possibles." I was ready to jump into the game head first.

The next morning I woke up bright and early. I was so amped up my mother didn't know what was wrong with me.

"Why are you so energized today?" she asked as she passed me ten dollars in spending money.

"I went to bed early last night. Thanks, Mom. I gotta go. I have a test," I said before kissing her on the cheek and running out of the door.

I ran the three blocks to Horse's house and walked in. I never had to knock on their door. I was pretty much family. Nate and Horse were upstairs in Nate's room.

"Yo, what's good. I'm here," I said, out of breath.

"Nigga, sit down before your ass pass out. Why the hell are you breathing so damn hard?" Horse asked.

"I wanted to make sure I got here on time. Had to make a good impression."

"That's good. I like that," Nate said as he sat on the bed separating some small bags of weed. "A'ight, these bags are all nickel bags. Make sure you sell these full price. I wouldn't care if yo' momma was buying a bag. She gets that shit for five dollars, you understand?"

"Perfectly," I said, nodding my head. My eyes were as wide as a kid's in Toys "R" Us.

"All right, we gotta go, Nate, so we ain't late. They start tripping when we come in late and shit," Horse said, passing Nate his backpack. "Give him your bag," Horse said.

Nate filled both of our backpacks with equal amounts of bags, 200 each. To some people that wasn't a lot, but when you're struggling that shit is like a million dollars. We headed out and walked into the building and made our way to our first period classes. After each class, I approached the people I knew were guaranteed sales, and just like that, the bags began to disappear. I could barely pay attention in class I was so focused on getting rid of the work. By 1:30 p.m., I was down to fewer than ten bags. I had the gift of gab, and I was blessed with a hustle that was unmatched by any nigga my age. I guess I got that from my bitch-ass father. At least I could thank him for that.

I met up with Horse in the hallway right before last period.

"What's good, Horse. How many bags you got left?"

"Man, I don't know. A lot," he said, looking like a sad-ass puppy dog. "What about you?"

"I'm all out," I said with a huge smile on my face.

"Word? All of it is gone? Man, how the fuck did you do that?"

"Nigga, you know I could sell ice to a Eskimo." I laughed. "Let's run in the bathroom and I'll take some from you and sell them for you."

By the end of the day I had sold another twenty of his bags. It's amazing how everybody wants to fit in. People who had never smoked in their lives were copping bags just to fit in with the in crowd. Horse was left with about fifty bags thanks to me. I couldn't wait to get back to Nate to show him how I moved. He was sure to be impressed with me.

We walked over to the block where Nate was sitting on the hood of his BMW with a beer can concealed in a brown paper bag. "What's up, li'l niggas?"

"I'm all out," I said, opening up my empty backpack to show him. I reached into the inside and pulled out the bills totaling $1,000. "Here you go, it's all here, one thousand."

"What about you?" Nate asked Horse.

"I got about fifty left."

"About fifty or fifty? I need an exact count," Nate said as he slid down off the car.

"I don't know exactly," Horse said.

"Man, sit down in the car and count that shit," Nate yelled.

Horse walked over and got inside the car. I stood and waited patiently. Nate stood silent for the next five minutes until Horse got out of the car.

"I have fifty-two bags left."

"So you're telling me you were only able to get rid of 148 bags all day?"

"Yeah," Horse replied with his head hung low.

You could tell that he was afraid of what would come next. He'd always looked up to his brother and talked about how he wanted to be just like him. I wished that I could've sold all of them for him just to avoid seeing him with the puppy dog face.

"You see, there are two types of people in the world: natural born leaders and natural followers. Clearly, you aren't the leader I thought you would be. Your man here, that's who you should strive to be like. The only way to get ahead in this business is to outsell your competition. Today was a test for just that. I wanted to see who I could trust to be a boss, and Dontay here has impressed me," he said as he passed me both the cash I'd given him as well as the cash Horse had. "For a job well done, all of this is yours."

"Really?" I asked, trying not to smile too hard.

"Yeah, really. Now that I see what you can do I will put you on to some major work. Tomorrow, meet me at the crib at the same time, and we'll talk."

"Okay, I'll be there with bells on, man. I appreciate this more than you know," I said. I reached out to give him a handshake.

"I'll talk to you later on," he said, looking over at Horse.

"All right." Horse walked behind me as we headed in the direction of the park. Once we were out of Nate's view I took the time to build his confidence back up.

"Don't worry, man. I promise that you'll always be good, trust me," I said as I took the money that he'd made for the day and put it in his hand.

"That's yours, man. I appreciate it, but I know how much you need it. It's all good."

"Nah, man, it's yours. You worked for it so take it."

"Thanks, man," he said, taking the money and putting it into his pocket.

"So what do you think he's going to say to you later?"

"I don't know, but ain't shit he could say that would make me feel worse than I do. I just wanted to make him proud."

"And you will. Stop beating yourself up. Just wait and see what he says."

By this time we were almost to the corner of my block. We gave each other handshakes and went our separate ways. Even though I felt bad for Horse, I was on cloud nine. I was looking forward to being in the game. I knew that trouble always lurked around the corner so I didn't expect things to be perfect. Either way, the way I felt at that moment was the way that I wanted to continue to feel.

Chapter Seven

Shit Changed

Desire

Shit changed for me following my brief encounter with Dontay, and not for the better. I always thought that losing Tyrese was the one terrible thing I'd go through in my lifetime. I mean, for sure I thought God would make the rest of my life a piece of cake after the trauma I'd been through.

It was graduation day, and I couldn't wait to get it over with. Finally, I was on my way to adulthood and free to do whatever the hell I wanted. I put on the all-white dress with strappy sandals that Lala had saved up to get. My hair had been pressed and bounced down to the middle of my back. I had my red and gold cap and gown in a garment bag while I waited in the rear hall of Liacouras Center. Lala had dropped me off and told me that she'd be back after she checked on my mother. My mother had been dealing with lung cancer and chemotherapy so my sister was primarily her caretaker. We used her social security and disability money to make ends meet. Shit was tight for us, and we never really recovered from the death of Tyrese. Lala couldn't get a job because she had to take care of us.

It was almost time for us to march when one of our school counselors came over and pulled me to the side.

"I need you to come with me," Ms. Marsh said when she approached.

I could tell by the look on her face that something was terribly wrong. "But we're just about to march. What's wrong?" I asked.

"Just come with me. I'll fill you in when we get outside."

I followed her, the whole time my stomach in knots. I didn't know what was happening or what awaited us at the door.

"Please, Ms. Marsh, tell me what's going on," I asked as we neared the front of the building.

She opened the door where Lala was standing with tears running down her cheeks. I stopped walking. I wasn't ready to hear any bad news, especially on my graduation day. I didn't want to hear what she had to say, but I knew I didn't have a choice.

"What is it? Just tell me," I said from the top of the stairs.

"She's gone, D," she said.

"Who?"

"Mom. When I went back home, she wasn't breathing. I called 911, but by the time they got there, she was already gone." She wept as she tried to tell me the details.

Was I wrong for not caring? She was my mother, yes, but really she didn't give a shit about me. At that moment I wanted to console my sister, I wanted to take her pain away, but all I could think about was my diploma. That piece of paper would be my ticket out of the fucked-up life I'd been given. Maybe it was best for all of us. Now Lala could actually have a life. If you asked me, she should've been thanking God for her freedom, because surely that had to be better than cleaning up her mother's vomit and shit every hour.

"Okay, now I need to go back inside. Graduation is starting," I replied with a stone face.

"D?" she yelled as I turned to walk toward the door.

"I have to go, Lala. She's dead. What the hell do you want me to do about it?"

"I want you to act like you care. Act like I just told you that our mother just died," she yelled.

"Correction: your mother just died. That hasn't been my mother in a very long time. I'm sorry, Lala, but I have to go. I'll see you back at home."

"Desire!" she yelled.

I didn't respond. I went inside, and got back in line just in time. I refused to let anything ruin my day. It's not like me going home at that moment would bring her back to life. I smiled as I walked across the stage and got my certificate. You would've never known that I'd just been given the news that would've broken even the toughest man to pieces.

After graduation was over I grabbed a ride with Octavia and her mom then walked home from their house. I was just turning the corner when a familiar vehicle drove by me. It was the same black Expedition that I'd seen Dontay get into that night at the lounge. The car slowed down, and then came to a complete stop in the middle of the block. I was nervous, but I continued walking down the block attempting to act as if I hadn't noticed the car. As I got closer, I saw the driver's side window roll down. Behind the wheel was the big nigga I'd seen Dontay with.

"Hey, come here for a second," he called out and waved his hand.

"Me?" I asked, pointing to my chest.

"I don't see nobody else out here," he replied.

I slowly walked over to the car. I stood far enough from the door so that I could haul ass if he tried to pull me inside.

"Yes?" I said as I stood holding my cap and gown over my arm.

"I've been looking for you for months. What's your name?"

"My name is D. Why were you looking for me?"

"Because a friend of mine wants to meet you. I'm sure you know Dontay."

"I know of him, yes, but why does he want to meet me?" I asked, trying to play it cool when in all actuality my stomach was doing flips.

"Listen, I'll let him tell you all that. Write your number down, and I'll pass it on to him," he said as he passed me a small piece of paper and an ink pen.

I wrote it down and handed it back to him.

"I know D isn't your full name, so what does the D stand for?"

"Desire."

"Desire? Is that right?" He chuckled. "All right, Miss Desire, you have a good day, a'ight? I'll pass this on."

"Okay," I said as he rolled up his window, and sped off. As soon as he was out of my view I laughed. "I knew it! I knew he noticed me," I said aloud.

As I approached my house, I noticed Lala sitting on the steps talking on the phone. "Let me call you back. She just got home," she said before ending her call.

"Hey," I said as I stopped on the side of the steps.

"Are you okay?" she asked.

"I'm good. Are you?"

"No, D, our mother just died. I'm fucked up right now. I really needed you to be here for me today, and you turned your back on me. You turned your back on our family."

"I needed to graduate. You know how important that was to me."

"You still would've graduated. You just wouldn't have walked down the aisle."

"It's not the same thing and you know it. I mean, after all of the shit that I've been through, you couldn't have just waited until it was over with to tell me?"

"I just can't believe how cold you have become. I really don't understand."

"Same way I couldn't believe how she didn't give a shit if I bled to death the day I was shot. All she cared about was her money train. If you can't see how I became who I am then maybe you never will. Look, I need to go change. I have a graduation party to attend," I said as I walked around her and went inside.

This time, she didn't try to stop me from walking away. I didn't know how else to explain it. I just didn't care, and I wanted her to stop trying to make me.

Chapter Eight

Watch the Throne

Dontay

2003 was the year that shit got real. By this time, I'd been working for Nate for nine years. I had my own crew and more than enough dough. I'd put my mother up in a big-ass five-bedroom house. She was driving a Mercedes-Benz CLK with a custom interior. As for Horse, he'd gone off to college and worked a nine to five. It was crazy how the tables had turned, because that was once my dream. A dream that was shattered the day my punk-ass daddy left us high and dry. I had everything that I wanted and, call me naïve but, I thought that nothing could go wrong. Little did I know, my whole world was about to be turned upside down.

It was midafternoon, and I'd just stopped by the spot when Nate stormed in with a ski mask in one hand and his gun in the other. I didn't know what the fuck had happened, but I knew it couldn't be good.

"Everybody out!" he yelled.

All of the niggas and women who were in the house packaging up the work headed for the door. I was on my way out behind them when he called me back.

"Nah, not you," he yelled.

I stopped and pushed the door closed. "What's up?"

"That muthafucker is dead," he yelled as he lit a cigarette and sat down at the table.

"Who?" I asked. He had a lot of enemies so it could've been a number of people.

"That nigga Reese from the north side. Followed that nigga to his crib and wet his ass up."

"Word?" I asked. Nate had beef with Reese for as long as I could remember. The beef began over a corner and escalated from that point. Nate didn't like being disrespected and even after he had words with Reese nothing changed. Reese was determined to keep his corner, which infuriated Nate. He'd put a hit out on him awhile back, but they'd be unsuccessful in the attempts to take him out.

"If you want shit done right you gotta do that shit yourself."

"I hear that. So you good? You need me to do anything?"

"Yeah, I'm good. Shit, my problem is solved."

"You need some extra security until shit calms?"

"Nah. That nigga was the only muthafucker bold enough to step to me. So I ain't got no worries." He laughed.

"A'ight, well, let me know if you need anything from me. I need to go make some rounds."

"Will do, and tell them to get back to work on your way out."

"A'ight. I'll talk to you later," I said before shaking his hand and leaving.

On the way around the city I felt uneasy. Granted, there were some niggas who just needed to be taken out, but Tyrese ran with a tight crew. I knew that shit wasn't over by a long shot. At every drop I was looking over my shoulder. I didn't trust anyone other than Nate and even that shit was suspect. I'd seen him murder his own friends and associates so I knew I wasn't exempt from his wrath. I pulled up to the last spot and two of the corner boys, Dontay and Rick, ran over to the car.

"Yo, they shot up Nate's spot, man!" Rick yelled as soon as I rolled down the window.

"What? I just left there," I yelled.

"They just called the crib and said Nate got hit. They were driving him to Hahnemann Hospital."

"Damn, man, what the fuck!" I yelled. "Y'all good here? I gotta go see what the fuck is going on."

"Yeah, I think we should shut down for the day."

"You're probably right. Go 'head and shut down, and I'll get up with y'all in a minute."

I drove off speeding through the streets. I couldn't even think straight. I would've never expected a retaliation to come so swiftly. I prayed that he would pull through as I made my way down to the emergency room. When I pulled up, my heart sank into the pit of my stomach. I saw some of the strongest niggas breaking down in tears. Immediately, I knew he hadn't made it. I couldn't even get out of the car as I sat and watched. I thought about that fact that I had just left him. A few more minutes and I'd have been laid up next to him. I tried to get my thoughts together before I got out, when I heard a loud scream followed by a bunch of commotion. I looked out the window to my left and saw Horse being held by a few security guards. I jumped out of the car and ran over to him.

"I got him," I said to the one guard. The guard looked at me like I was crazy. "I said I got him," I yelled at the security guard.

The bigger security guard looked over at me with evil eyes before backing away. Once they let go I grabbed Horse and hugged him. Though I wasn't related to them by blood they were the closest thing to a family I had. I could feel his heartbreak and shared his devastation. Our brother was gone.

"I'm gonna kill whoever is responsible for this shit!" he yelled as I held on to him. I knew if I let him go he'd tear up some shit. He'd been known for taking out his anger on anything that wasn't nailed down. I couldn't even think of any words to say. I knew that nothing I said would comfort him. I wanted to answer his question at that moment and let him know about the conversation that I'd had with Nate just before this shit went down, but I decided that now wasn't the best time. After a few more seconds, he calmed down enough that I was confident in letting him go.

"Let's ride out," Horse said.

"A'ight," I agreed and walked around to the driver's side of my car.

Horse got in and closed the door. "They wouldn't even let me see him," he said, shaking his head in disgust.

I couldn't even respond. I wanted to allow him to grieve without dealing with the shit that was on my mind. I knew that it would be pointless to go after the niggas who did it, because their boss was dead. Without Tyrese they wouldn't have a leg to stand on. Instead of going to war with a bunch of minions, we needed to plan for takeover. In my mind I was playing out the moves I needed to make. I was the only one who could continue in Nate's place. He'd put me on to everything he knew, he'd introduced me to his Colombian connect and given me the combinations to all of the safes. I even had the key to his house, something that Horse never had.

"So what's next? I know he'd want you to run shit in his absence," Horse said.

"I don't want you to worry about that shit right now, man. You need to be with your family."

"You are my family. I'm worried about you, too. I don't need to worry about burying you next."

"You won't. I'll get everything under control. I promise you that."

"Well, I'll step up to the plate if need be. Fuck working for the white man. I'll work for you."

"All right. I'll keep that in mind. Did you want me to drop you off somewhere? I'm gonna go make sure everything is shut down for the night."

"Nah, I'll ride with you."

"Cool," I replied.

I had so many thoughts and emotions running through me at that moment. I'd wanted to be the boss for a long time, but never this way. I would've wanted to rule side by side with Nate. I knew that I could do anything that I put my mind to so I was sure that I could handle it. I'd watched the throne for years. Now it was time to take a seat and do things my way.

Chapter Nine

Better Be Good

Desire

I walked into the party with a big smile on my face. Shany's mom had gone all out for this celebration. They'd rented a banquet hall, and decorated it with our school colors. I was going to try my hardest to have a good time despite all of the drama going on in my life. I spoke to a few of my classmates as I walked to the back where I could see my friends standing in a small circle.

"Hey, ladies," I said as I approached.

"Hey, girl. I thought you wasn't going to make it," Shany said, reaching out to give me a hug.

"Girl, I wouldn't miss this party for the world. Besides, I have something to tell you."

"What, girl?"

"Walk over here with me," I said, nodding my head to the left.

"I'll be right back, y'all," Shany told the group. "This better be good," she said.

"Remember that day when we were over at the lounge and we saw Dontay getting into that black truck?"

"Yeah."

"Well, I was on my way walking home and that same car stopped me. The big guy we'd seen with Dontay asked for my number and said that Dontay wanted to meet me," I said with a girlish giggle.

"What? Girl, how do you know it was really for Dontay? What if that big-ass ugly nigga wanted the digits for himself?"

"I hadn't even thought about that," I said.

"Well, I hope that isn't the case, 'cause, girl, I would vomit for you if that shit was a lie. No way could I ever get close to that dude." She burst into laughter.

"Well, we will surely see. Now let's get to the party and have some fun."

Soon Octavia arrived and we had a ball. We danced, celebrating our future. The party was over at nine, and I dreaded going home. I just didn't feel like being bothered. I took my time walking down the block. I was so deep in thought that I almost didn't notice the black Mercedes parked on the corner with the music blasting. Leaning on the side of the hood was Dontay.

In one hand was a beer and in the other a phone. He was chatting away until I got close, when he abruptly ended his call. I wanted to fake it and try to be cool as if I hadn't noticed him standing there. He was fine as shit and simply irresistible. Everything about him was perfection, a true masterpiece. He was dressed from head to toe in designer gear. I could only imagine the price tag associated with his outfit. I was mesmerized, so much so I could see his lips moving, but couldn't hear a thing.

"Hello, is anybody in there?" he said while waving his hands in front of me.

"Yes, I'm sorry. I've had a really long day. Hi," I said, holding in my smile.

"Well, I've been looking for you. Desire, right?"

"Yes, that's me."

"When I heard that was your name I couldn't believe it. I wondered what was behind it. It's truly one of the most unique names I've ever heard, besides on a stripper, and I'm sure you aren't one of those, are you?"

I laughed. "No, I am definitely not one of those."

"Well, that's a good thing. Can't have my lady up there on no stripper pole shaking her ass for dollars."

"Your lady?" I asked, shocked by the claim.

"Well, not yet, but you will be," he said with confidence.

"From what I hear, you have a woman. So I don't see how that would even be possible."

"Where did you hear that?"

"I mean, everyone knows you, and the streets talk."

"The streets? What do you know about the streets?" he said as he laughed.

"I know a little bit," I said with one hand on my hip.

"I find that hard to believe. You're too pretty to be in the streets."

"So is it true?"

"Is what true?"

"That you have a woman." I wanted him to answer that with a no. I would've been crushed had he said yes. I hadn't heard anything on the streets about him having a woman. I just needed a clever way to ask the question. I didn't want him to know that I'd practically stalked him trying to get his attention.

"Yes and no," he replied.

"What does that mean?"

"It means just that: yes and no."

"That answer doesn't make any sense," I said with a twisted lip. I wasn't sure what he was trying to hide, but I needed to know the answer.

"It makes perfect sense if think about it."

"I am thinking, and it should be yes or no, not both."

"Well, the answer to that depends on you."

"Huh? If you aren't going to be honest there is no need to continue this conversation." I was clueless. I had no idea what the hell he was trying to say.

"Truth is, I have a woman, but she just doesn't know it yet."

By this time, he was standing so close to me I could feel his breath. The smell of his cologne was sending chills up and down my spine. He was arousing all of my senses without even touching me. He was as close to perfect as one could possibly get. I held my composure as best I could. I had never been this up close and personal with a man, and I say "man" because there wasn't anything boyish about him. For a second, I thought he was going to kiss me—well, at least I hoped that he would. I closed my eyes, waiting to feel his lips touch mine, but there was nothing.

"In due time, baby girl, in due time," he said as he backed away.

He smiled as he walked around to the driver's side and hopped in. I stood there watching him drive away, confident that one day that would be my man. I walked home and walked past all of the relatives and family friends who were piled in the living room. I went up to my room, shut the door, and grabbed the phone off the table. I dialed Shany. Octavia would never be happy for me so I didn't think to call her and share the news. For whatever reason, Octavia didn't believe a man like Dontay would ever look twice at me. At one point in time, I would've believed that too, but a lack of confidence won't get you nowhere. I was anxious for Shany to pick up so I could spill the tea.

"Hello," she said, sounding exhausted.

"Girl, guess who I saw on my way home?" I yelled.

"Girl, why the hell are you so loud? Who did you see?"

"Sorry, I'm just excited. As I turned the block, I see none other than Dontay with his sexy ass, standing there leaning up against the car. I think he was waiting on me."

"For real? What did he say?"

"He said that I was his woman, but I just didn't know it yet."

"He really said that?"

"Yes, girl. I'm still on cloud nine. I would've never thought that he would be interested in me."

"Why not? You are gorgeous. A man would have to be blind not to notice that."

"That's why I called you, 'cause Octavia would never agree," I said, feeling reassured.

"That's because deep down Octavia wishes that she was you. I mean, she's my girl and all and she has a nice body, but that's about it. A fat ass will only get you so far."

"Well, I'm about to get ready to go to bed. I just wanted to let you what happened. I'll see you tomorrow, girl."

"All right, girl. See you tomorrow," she replied.

I took a shower and jumped straight in bed. I kept my door locked that night to avoid being bothered.

Chapter Ten

Did You See Her?

Dontay

I wanted to make her sweat just a little. You had to be careful with young girls because they couldn't control their emotions. I'd learned to slow walk them into my life. You couldn't give them too much at once or things could quickly get out of control. I had my mind made up. She was already mine. I just needed to test her to make sure that was the right move to make. She was special, and even though I didn't know her well, I could tell just by looking at her. She was pure, not tainted by a train of niggas running up in her. She was the type you get and keep forever.

I had a lot to do this particular day. I had to meet with a new supplier who was giving me a much better price on pure cocaine. I stood to make triple what I did now, and I was looking forward to it. I drove down to the suite where Horse and the crew had been patiently waiting for me. Horse greeted me at the door with our signature handshake.

"What's good? Is everybody here?"

"Yeah, they are all here except that nigga Joe Joe. I tried to call him a few times. I even sent Jay and them to look for him earlier. He came back and said he couldn't find him."

"Well, we'll deal with that shit later," I said as I walked into the room filled with my most trusted soldiers. In this game you had to be careful who you shared certain information with. There was always someone watching and waiting for the right time to try to take your spot.

"So what's the deal?" Jay was the first one to speak.

"I brought you all here today to talk about a new connect. I know I've been working with Manny for a few years and the quality is great. It's the price that I have an issue with. I found a new supplier from Miami who has pure cocaine for almost sixty percent less than what I pay now. The reason I called this meeting is because I wanted to make sure we could move the weight since a better quality product with a cheaper price tag will bring more customers. I don't want to take on more than we are capable of handling."

"I get what you're saying, but how do you know the cocaine is pure? I mean, why not do a test run first and see what the response is before cutting ties with Manny and investing in something that you don't know for a fact will work?"

"I know it's pure because I tested it already. This isn't something that I just decided on overnight. This is something that has been in the works for a very long time. I've always looked at you all as partners. I need to be sure that all of you are on board before moving forward."

Everyone except Jay was silent. Probably all in deep thought. I was never one to bring something to that table that I didn't think would work. I wasn't here for permission. I just wanted them to feel like they had a say.

"I mean, if you think it'll work I'm down. Anything that can put us in a better position is all right with me. I didn't get into this game to be a corner boy. I got into it to be a boss. So, I'm wit' it," Jay said.

"Well, you know I'm definitely with it," Horse said.

"All right, well, I have some shit to handle, and I'm going to meet with the new connect by the end of the week. I'll update you all once I have everything lined up. Cool?"

Everyone agreed before we all went our separate ways. Horse and I chatted briefly before we left. There were things I could tell Horse that I wouldn't dare tell anyone else. He was the closest thing to a brother I had. Whether it was relationships, life, or death, he always had my back. He was always supportive of my decisions even when they may not have been the smartest.

"When you find out what's up with Joe Joe hit me up. I need to do some personal shit, but I won't be far if you need me."

"Is everything good?"

"Yeah, everything is good," I replied as we walked toward the elevator that led to the parking garage.

"You sure?"

"Yeah, man, I'm sure." I laughed. "If things weren't good, trust me, I would definitely let you know."

"All right, just checking, 'cause I know you. You just seem like you have a lot on your mind right now."

"I do, but nothing you need to worry about. I'll update you later for sure."

"All right. Well, I'll call you when I find out about Joe Joe," he said, reaching out to shake my hand. After we parted ways, I got in my car and drove off.

For the past few months I'd been going to the same spot and sitting for hours watching. I'd found out where Jimmy Black lived, and I grew angrier almost every day. It didn't matter how many years had passed, I was still furious. I wanted him to pay for what he did to my mother, for what he did to us. He didn't deserve the shit that he had, and I wanted to be the one to snatch it right from under his feet.

Almost every day I sat in the car like I was on a police stakeout watching how he ran his operation. I watched where he went at what time. I knew what time he went to bed at night. Hell, I could even tell you what kind of toothpaste he used. I'd studied him like a book. Every day by his side was his son, Lamar. I would never understand how a man could be a great dad to one child but not give a shit about the other one simply because of the women who gave birth to them. The day he walked out, I thought about how many ways I could murder him. Every night when I went to sleep I saw visions of watching him take his last breath. I became a ruthless killer because of him. Each murder was practice for the ultimate kill. Every time I pulled the trigger, I envisioned his face.

I sat in the car in deep thought, checking my surroundings. There were people going in and out of their homes and some random children playing in the street. An hour had passed before I finally saw my father appear. He stepped out of a white Mercedes CLS500. You could tell that it was freshly washed because the white paint was so shiny it looked wet. As usual, Lamar stepped out of the passenger seat. Most people would assume that the rage I felt was triggered by jealousy, but it wasn't. Unless you've been in my shoes you couldn't begin to speculate.

I watched them enter the corner store, and I waited a half hour until they returned to the sidewalk. They stood outside the car chatting while I watched. I could've taken him out right at that moment, but I decided against it. It wasn't the right time. I started my car and pulled out of the parking spot. I didn't bother rolling down the windows. I wanted them to wonder who was behind the slow-moving car with dark tinted windows. Both of them turned and stared, trying to see who was behind the wheel. I was just about to a complete stop before I quickly drove off. I was sure that they got a glimpse of my personalized plate. I'd see them again, real soon.

Chapter Eleven

Started from the Bottom

Tracy

2003

At fifteen I had a body like Tyra Banks and the men would drool when I walked down the block. My mother always told me that it was okay for men to look, but if they wanted to touch, they had to pay. I wasn't about to be a prostitute, but as I got older, I understood exactly where she was coming from. My virginity was stolen from me, and the painful memory of it was something that I tried to erase from my mind. Travis was the name of the man who held me down and forced me to have sex with him. The experience didn't last very long, but it left a part of me aching, and there wasn't anything that could take the pain away. The worst part of it all was the fact that he was my mother's man, and I was afraid to tell her because I feared her reaction. I knew that it would make her choose between the two of us, and losing him meant she would lose money. I decided to keep it a secret, and it was because of that that it continued.

Though Travis was her man, eventually he was mine too, and I began to enjoy it. He would give me money just as often as he would give it to her. On afternoons when she would be out shopping he would be at home with me.

It was during this time I learned the value of what I had. I discovered the methods my mother tried to teach me. Some would probably say that it was wrong to continue the relationship, but I used him exactly the way that he'd used me, and I wasn't the least bit sorry for it. Travis was also a teacher, not certified, but he was the one who taught me everything I knew about sex. It's because of him that I knew how to satisfy a man. The craziest thing was how we were able to keep it a secret from my mom even after he dumped her for me. I can remember the day that it happened as if it was yesterday. My mother wasn't all that affected by it since she'd already had suspicions he was having an affair. I had just come home from school and as I walked through the hallway that led to our two-bedroom apartment I could hear them yelling obscenities at each other. Instead of going in I stood at the door and listened.

"You know what? Fuck you, Travis. I already knew you were fucking somebody else so that shit isn't a surprise!" she screamed.

"Good! Because I can't deal with your tired ass anymore! I got me some young pussy now!"

"Just finish gathering your shit up and get out. I'm not going to keep being disrespected!" she continued to scream.

"If I gathered all of my shit you wouldn't have anything in here. Did you forget I bought almost everything in this muthafucker?"

"Take what you want. I'll get it again!"

"Don't worry about it, you can keep it. I wouldn't want Tracy to be in here without. You're lucky you have her!" he said, walking toward the door.

I instantly scrambled to find a hiding spot in the hall. I didn't want either of them to know that I had been eavesdropping. As he opened the door, he turned to look at her one last time before shaking his head and walking out. In a way, I was glad that I wouldn't have to share him with her any longer. I know that it sounds bad, but I had grown so attached to him, and seeing him with her only made me sick.

After I heard him leave the building I headed into the apartment. My mother was sitting at the table smoking a cigarette while talking on the phone. I waved hello as I headed to my bedroom, and within a few minutes a page came through my pager. I didn't recognize the number so I used my private line and dialed it with caution.

"Hello!" the deep-toned voice spoke on the other end.

"Hi. Did someone page Tracy?" I asked since I didn't recognize the voice either.

"Yeah, hold on."

"Hello!" Another male voice came through a few seconds later.

"Travis?" I asked.

"Hey, baby, what's up?"

"Nothing much. What's up with you?" I said quietly, since I didn't want my mother to hear my conversation.

"I moved out today, and I want to see you tonight!"

"I don't know if I can sneak out. She might know," I said nervously.

"She'll be out tonight. You know it's Tuesday. She hangs out with her friends. I'll pick you up around ten. Just stay by the phone."

"Okay."

"Wear something sexy for me, too. Something to show that frame of yours."

I agreed as I slowly hung up the phone. I could hear my mother's footsteps as they neared my room. I figured that she might have heard me on the phone or wanted to let me in on the dissolution of her relationship with Travis. She turned the knob without knocking, and I tried to look as if I was straightening up my bed.

She looked around the room before speaking. "Who were you on the phone with?" she asked as she placed her hand on her hip.

"I was talking to Trina about a homework assignment!" I lied.

"I put that lying-ass nigga out today, so you won't be seeing him around here anymore!" she said, taking a puff of her cigarette. "I have to go out tonight and hustle me another man, since the bills damn sure won't pay themselves!"

I continued to sit there silently, waiting for her to leave the room. She stood there for a few more seconds before speaking again. "And you need to clean up more than that bed. This room is a wreck!" She turned to leave the room without closing the door behind her.

I quickly got up off of the bed and pushed it shut before practically jumping for joy. It would be a piece of cake getting out tonight since she wouldn't be here. Now all I had to do was settle on an outfit and wait for her to leave. I quickly began to rummage through my dresser, throwing clothes all over. I was determined to blow Travis's mind.

It wasn't long before I was in a full relationship with Travis. Eventually, my mother found out and put me out, and I had no other choice but to run to him. Things weren't perfect, but they were okay. I had a roof over my head, and I didn't have to deal with my mother. That was until Travis found another woman and decided to put me out.

After Travis threw me out, I had to find a place to stay. Luckily my girl Karen had the coolest mom on earth and allowed me to move in with them until I was able to get back on my feet. Going back to my mom's was definitely out of the question. Besides, even if I wanted to go back she wouldn't allow it. She felt that I had committed the ultimate betrayal by sleeping with Travis. Never mind the fact that he had raped me in the beginning. All that mattered to her was that I screwed up her cash flow, fuck everything else.

I didn't let the breakup get me down since I was too fine for that. At seventeen I was envied by all of the neighborhood chicks, and I loved it. I was the bitch everyone loved to hate. Shit, even my mother was jealous, since she knew she'd never be young again and, in a nutshell, that meant she would never be me.

The months flew by, and it was almost my eighteenth birthday. Since my birthday was on a Wednesday we decided to celebrate the weekend before. Karen and me shopped all day to find the sexiest outfits since I planned on snagging me a man that night. I was tired of fucking the young hustlers from the projects to get money. I needed to move on to bigger and better things. The outfit I settled on was sure to make every guy in the place drool. The dress was short and hugged my ass so tight it looked like I was wearing body paint. After shopping, we headed to the neighborhood check cashing place, where we could get hooked up with a fake ID. The cashier, a Puerto Rican girl named Nina, was known for giving anyone with dough a fake ID, but since Karen and her were cool, she gave us ours for free.

I was excited as we headed down to Center City to the club called Pinnacle. It was known to be packed on Saturdays, and I had a feeling tonight would be my night. After waiting in the long-ass line to get in, we paid our fifteen-dollar cover fee and entered the club. We decided to take a Polaroid before we started partying, because after I got a couple of drinks, I was sure to forget all about it.

The club was packed from front to back, and after I had a couple shots of Hennessy, I danced all night long. I gave

my number to a few guys, but none of them really seemed
like the baller I was looking for. You could never really
tell, so I would have to chat with them after tonight to see
if they were worthy of my time. Once the lights came on,
that was our cue to head outside.

I was still tipsy from the alcohol, but you couldn't tell
by the way I switched down the street toward the parking
lot. A few guys tried to holla, but none of them really
sparked my interest. As we turned the corner toward
the lot, there was a group of guys standing on the corner
passing out flyers. I tried not to look at anyone directly.
Hell, I couldn't really see clearly anyway.

As we walked past, one guy grabbed me by the arm.
"Hey, what's up. Do you have a number I can call you at?"
he said, getting straight to the point.

"Yeah," I said, smiling as he took out his cell phone to
enter the number.

"What's your name?" he asked, moving close to me.

"Tracy!" I said as I tried to stand still hoping I didn't
appear as drunk as I felt.

"Okay, Tracy, I'm going to call you."

"Okay," I said as I walked away.

I couldn't remember what the hell he said his name
was, but the next morning, I looked at the flyer and
noticed the name. "Dontay!" I said aloud. Damn, he was
fine. He stood well over six feet tall and had this serious
look on his face that turned me on.

We were heading down to Old City that night so I
talked Karen into stopping by his party so I could get
another look at him. He was standing outside when we
walked up to the club. I headed over to him to say hello.

"Hey, you made it. Thanks for showing some love!"
he said as he leaned in to give me a hug—and damn, it
felt good. We headed inside for a while but ended up
leaving early to go to the party we originally came out for.

I didn't care. I had gotten to see Dontay again, if only for a few minutes. This was the start of my relationship with the man I'd later marry. He was a savior. Without him, I probably would've ended up homeless. Most people wondered why I would stay with a man like him, but it was simple. He took damn good care of me, and dealing with all of his affairs was the sacrifice for a better life.

Chapter Twelve

And So We Meet Again

Dontay

I let another week go by before I called Desire. By then, she'd probably thought that I was no longer interested. To be honest, I had been busy handling business. Everything had gone well in Miami and everything was falling into place, just as I had planned. Now, it was back to my next project. I pulled up near the corner of her block and parked at the corner. I dialed her number.

"Hello," a female voice spoke. I could tell it wasn't her, but instead a more mature woman.

"Hi, is Desire available? This is Dontay," I said, revealing my identity without being asked.

"How old are you, Dontay? Because you sound a little too old to be calling for my sister."

"Well, you certainly can't tell how old someone is by the sound of their voice, but to answer your question, I'm not that much older than your sister. Maybe I can come meet you in person to make you more comfortable. How about that?"

"Yeah, well, we'll see about that, Mr. Dontay. Hold on, all right?" she said.

I could hear her calling for Desire, and a few moments later I heard her voice. There was just something about hearing it that was music to my ears.

"Hello."

"Hey, baby, it's Dontay."

"Baby? I haven't even heard from you since the day you were standing on my block. You got my hopes all up and then disappeared just as fast as you showed up."

"I got your hopes up? What did I say or do that got your hopes up or, better yet, crushed them?"

"You told me that I was your lady, that I was your woman. I expected to hear from you. It's bad enough I already have low self-esteem as it is."

"Listen, I was out of town. I had some things to handle, but I'm back now. Now that I'm back, we're going to work on that self-esteem, because we can't have that."

"So when will I see you?"

"Believe it or not, I'm closer than you think."

"What does that mean?"

"Look out your window and you'll see."

I could see her peeking out of the miniblinds. "What are you doing sitting outside of my house? Are you stalking me?"

"I can disappear again you know," I said as I laughed.

"No, I don't want that. I was just joking. Do you want me to come outside?" she asked in her girlish tone.

"Nah, I'll call you tomorrow. I just wanted to check on you. Sleep tight, all right?" I said before ending the call. I started the car and drove off.

I was just about to head home when my phone rang. It was Tracy. What started out as a casual booty call had blossomed into so much more. Tracy was one of those women who would allow another woman in your bed rather than let you go. I thought that was one of the reasons why I'd dealt with her as long as I had.

Now, let's be clear, she was easy on the eyes. She was about five foot six with a small waist and a round ass. Of course, she always looked immaculate courtesy of my bankroll. I felt I had no choice but to marry her. I knew I'd never find another chick like her. Our relationship was unconventional at times. We hadn't always stayed under the same roof. I was always busy so she knew there would be nights when I wouldn't make it home. I'd always been honest with her about other women, but this time, with Desire, I found myself hiding it. I was positive that she wouldn't be too happy about it. She was okay with a casual screw, but this was far from that. I would break it to her when the time was right. Since nothing was set in stone I still had time.

"Hey, babe, where are you?" she asked as soon as I picked up.

"In the car on my way home. What's up?"

"I wanted to see you. I miss you. I thought you were coming here right after you got back from Miami."

"I tried, but I had some other things I needed to handle that took longer than I anticipated."

"It's okay, I understand."

"I'm not that far from there, so give me a few minutes and I'll swing by."

"Okay, I'll be waiting."

It would be too hard, too much drama, to avoid her, so I figured it was best to just go ahead and get it over with. I went over to her house and used my key. The house was dark. I damn near tripped trying to maneuver through the house.

"Tracy," I called as I stood at the bottom of the steps. I could hear the faint sounds of a radio playing. It wasn't easy for me to identify the lyrics, but I could tell from where I was standing that it was mood music.

I started walking up the stairs and saw the bedroom door cracked open. There were flutters of light coming through. The closer I got I could hear moaning. I knew she was a huge fan of porn so I expected to open the bedroom door to find her watching TV or better yet playing with her pussy to get it ready for me. I pushed the door open and, just as I'd expected, she was lying there watching porn, ass naked. I never had to ask for sex with her. I never had to beat around the bush. She was always willing to give it to me whenever I wanted it.

I stood there watching her body glistening under the candlelight with her legs spread apart. She had two fingers inside of her pussy while her other hand squeezed her breast. It looked so good I almost didn't want to interrupt. I stood and watched for a few more moments until I couldn't take it anymore. I began to take off my clothes right in the doorway. There was a trail of my things leading up to the side of the bed. She was so deep into her masturbation that she hadn't even noticed that I'd been in the room. I stood there with my dick in my hand stroking it while I watched. Soon, she'd hit her climax and once she opened her eyes, my dick was already at eye level waiting for her to give it some attention. She reached up and grabbed hold of it without saying a word. She showed me just how much she'd missed me.

Tracy

After reaching an orgasm I opened my eyes, and was surprised to find Dontay standing in front of me naked holding his rock hard dick in his hand. I slowly got up from the bed, stood in front of him and grabbed hold of it. I backed him up against the wall so I could get to work. I whispered in his ear before slowly sticking my tongue out and licking his right earlobe. His dick began to grow rapidly and pulsate immediately. I moved my tongue from his ear, tracing a slippery path to his neck while using both hands to caress his hardness. I rubbed my fingers across the head of his dick, wiping away the remnants of pre-cum that formed a small puddle on top of it, and then I took those fingers into my mouth to suck it off. I moaned aloud while gently nudging him back toward the wall.

His voice quivered as I squatted and placed his ten-inch dick deep into my mouth and toward my throat. I was focused as I used one hand to jerk his dick, the other to massage his balls, and my tongue to suck the head in a circular motion. His head was leaned back against the wall while his hands were firmly gripping the back of my head. I could see him biting his lower lip trying to keep his composure as long as he could. I had been told in the past how great of a blowjob I could give, but I always strived to top that. If I could make a man's entire body shake while releasing his juices in my mouth I'd done my job, but if I could make that same man damn near cry trying to hold it all together so as not to appear weak, I'd achieved my goal.

At this moment satisfying him wasn't really my plan although it would be almost impossible for him not to be satisfied after receiving all of this loving I had to give. Since I was extremely horny, I was bound to ride him like a trained horse jockey and bust all over his pants.

"You like that?" I questioned with a sweet whisper, now using both hands to simultaneously stroke his dick. I would spit on it every few seconds to keep it moist as I massaged the head with my full lips and magical tongue. I could tell that he was holding in his moans as he took a slight gasp for air every few seconds. "What's the matter, cat got your tongue?" I asked playfully, though I knew it was more so the kung fu grip I had on him.

"Slow down, girl, you're gonna make me cum," he replied as his left hand gripped the side of the dresser and his right hand was firmly palming the back of my head.

My goal definitely wasn't to achieve premature ejaculation so I listened to his request and slowed down my pace just enough to keep him aroused.

I stood up from my squatting position and with one hand still firmly wrapped around his stiff penis I moved in close so that we were face to face, and I kissed him on the lips. He obliged and hungrily stuck his tongue into my mouth and swiftly massaged mine with his. I released my grip and used both hands to press on his shoulders, guiding him down to the cherry-wood floor. Without hesitation he took my cue and was lying down on the floor with his dick pointed straight in the air still stiff as wood. I was now standing over him and before squatting to make contact, I took two of my fingers and put them near my mouth. I gathered up spit and let it drip from my lips onto the tips of my index and middle fingers. Using the saliva as lubricant I rubbed my fingers across my clit then guided them into my pussy. I was staring him in the face as I bit my bottom lip and finger fucked myself for a minute while he stroked his dick and returned my stare.

"Come on and sit on this dick," he said while still stroking his dick up and down.

Without a response I squatted down and used my right hand to guide his dick inside of me. It immediately filled my walls and tickled my G-spot. "Oh shit, this feels good," I moaned as I almost erupted from the feeling of a warm piece of meat. Though I was a little out of practice, just like riding a bike once you learn how to ride a dick you never forget. With my feet planted on the floor, I rocked and swirled my hips at a steady pace tapping my clit with my fingers. "Is this pussy good to you?" I asked, though I knew for certain he was enjoying the pleasure that I was giving him.

"Yes, this pussy is magnificent," he replied with his hands on one ass cheek each guiding me up and down. I felt like all of the built-up adrenaline was finally flowing free and as my ass slapped up against him I could hear all of my juices and my pussy walls making a sucking sound.

"Ooooooh, shit, girl," was what he muttered as I picked up speed and swirled my hips faster. I could feel myself nearing an orgasm and as much as I wanted this encounter to last.

"Ooooooh," I yelled as my body began to shake, my legs began to tremble beneath me, and the cum that had been bottled up inside of me was slowly oozing down the shaft of his dick. After reaching that peak of sensitivity where your body shakes uncontrollably with every movement, I got up off of him so that he could stand. I got down on my knees in front of him once again and placed his dick in my mouth. This time, I needed him to release his load so I was working overtime to make sure that he did just that. I continued to suck him off, and I didn't let go. I used every dick sucking technique that I had ever seen, done, or heard of.

"Oh, shit. Oh, shit. I'm gonna cum," he yelled.

I released his dick from my lips, and he quickly began to jerk it back and forth. "Open your mouth," he said, intertwined with a moan. I opened my mouth and stuck my tongue out, and he released all of his cum in and around my mouth. I moaned with him and rubbed the remnants of his cum off with my fingers and then licked them with my tongue. "Damn, that was intense," he said as he looked down at me.

Chapter Thirteen

Charge It to the Game

Alisha

2006

"Your total is $4,565.95," the female cashier said. "Will that be cash or charge?"

"Cash," Desi said, pulling a wad of cash from his left pocket. He peeled off hundred after hundred, and passed it to the cashier. She looked at him in shock probably assuming that he was a criminal.

In this case, her assumption was right. Desi was a criminal, a drug lord to be exact. Shit, my man was doing damn good in the business, too. I didn't need for anything, but a bitch was spoiled so I wanted just about everything I saw. I couldn't help it. He'd made me that way. After the cashier counted and marked each bill to be sure they were legit, she handed Desi my bags, and we were on our way.

"Thank you, baby," I said, kissing him on the cheek.

"It ain't shit. You know I'd do anything for you." He smiled.

"So what's next?" I asked.

We were in New York City for our two-year anniversary. We walked out of Bergdorf Goodman and made our way to the garage where he'd parked. "Damn, can you just be surprised for once?"

"You know I hate surprises. I like to know what I'm walking into."

"You gotta chill, babe, seriously. I got this." He smiled, and grabbed a hold of my hand.

I loved this man more than any other man in my life. We'd had our rough times, but nothing that would make me leave him. Sure, he'd cheated, but what man doesn't? I'd worked too hard for this relationship to let another bitch steal him away.

"Okay, since today is a special one, I'm going to trrr-ryyyyy to sit on my hands." I laughed.

He knew just as well as I did that wasn't possible. I always spoke my mind, and it never mattered to me whether you wanted to hear what I had to say or not. Hell, when I first met Desi I was fighting a chick in a neighborhood bar. I wasn't liked by too many people, especially women, mostly because all of their men wanted me. I couldn't help it. I'd always been a bad bitch, but I could also hold my own. I was trashing this chick when a pair of strong arms pulled me off of her. Desi ushered me out of the bar and into his car to avoid being picked up by the cops. We'd been together ever since.

He turned on his radio and immediately began bobbing his head to the music. Jay-Z's *The Black Album* filled every inch of the car. I laid my head back on the headrest and glanced out of the window, hoping I could figure out where we were headed.

Within twenty minutes we arrived at the upscale Chinese restaurant Mr. Chow. I'd never eaten there before, but I'd heard about it being a hot spot for celebrities. I smiled as we entered the restaurant that was filled with tables all covered in white tablecloths. There was a man off to the side putting on a show, making noodles with his hands. I was excited. I didn't know what else Desi had planned, but I was anxious to find out. We were seated at a small table and immediately taken care of.

"Desi, what are you doing?" I asked.

He was far from romantic. He was more the type to throw you hush money.

"What do you mean? I can't take my woman out someplace special?"

"It's just not like you, so I'm just trying to figure out what you are up to."

Where I was from, people only did nice things for you when they wanted something or they were trying to make up for some foul shit they'd done. I hoped that it wasn't the latter. It was hard being optimistic with my background. I wasn't handed anything. Everything that I'd achieved I'd gone through a heap of shit to gain.

"Well, I bought you another gift. You wanna see it?"

"Of course I wanna see it!"

Just then the waiter came over to the table, and set a small box down in front of me. "For you, miss," he said before smiling and walking away.

"What is this?" I asked, afraid to touch it.

"Open it and see."

I picked up the box, and slowly opened it. I almost fainted when I was hit by the glistening of the huge diamond ring nestled inside of the box. In front of me was a yellow princess-cut diamond ring, at least five karats. I was afraid of it, and even more afraid of what it implied. Was this what I thought it was? I was in shock and speechless.

"Babe," he called out.

I was still silent as I admired the flawless stone.

"Babe," he called out once again.

"Yes," I replied, finally looking up from the box.

"So what do you say?"

"What do you mean? Are you asking me to marry you?" I asked, holding one hand on my chest, because I was sure I was about to go into cardiac arrest.

"That's exactly what I mean. You've been down wit' me since day one, and it's about time that we make it official."

I jumped up from my seat, and ran around to his. "Yes, baby, yes! I will marry you!" I screamed.

The patrons of the restaurant began clapping and whistling. I'd forgotten they were even there as I planted the most sensual kiss on his lips. I wanted to straddle him right there, but I contained my excitement. He took the box from my hand and removed the ring before placing it on my finger. I held it up in the air, and admired it some more. It was the most beautiful piece of jewelry I'd ever laid my eyes on. I couldn't imagine the price tag. I couldn't wait to get it appraised to see just how much he thought I was worth.

"Do you think we can get our food to go?" I whispered in his ear.

"To go? Babe, this is Mr. Chow not Mr. Lee on the corner." He laughed.

"Yes. I can't wait to show you how happy I am. I'm going to fuck you like it's the last piece I'll ever get."

He burst into laughter. "You are crazy, but that's why I love you." He leaned in to kiss me.

I got up off of his lap and went back to my seat. The waiter came and looked at us both crazy when we asked him to box the food up. I was sure he knew what that was about. Once our food was packaged, we headed to the parking garage. You couldn't slap the smile off my face. I was happier than I'd ever been in my life. I thought that I already had it all, but this was just the icing on the cake.

Once we began the drive to the hotel, I was quiet. I just wanted to reach the room and show him what I was working with. We reached the Four Seasons hotel in record time. I assumed he was as eager as I was. Inside the room there were roses laid out all over, a bottle of

Dom in the ice bucket, and chocolate-covered strawberries nearby. He'd gone all out for me. My mouth was wide open, filled with disbelief and amazement.

"Where is my man at? Because I'm convinced there is a stranger here," I asked as he walked up behind me and wrapped his arms around my waist. I felt secure in his arms as if our bond was forever. It felt unbreakable at that moment.

"I'm not your man anymore. I'm your fiancé and soon to be your husband," he whispered in my ear.

I turned around to face him and immediately leaned in for a kiss. Our tongues massaged each other's as his hands began to softly caress my lower back. My pussy was so moist I could feel the juices making their way to my upper thigh. As he moved closer, I could feel his dick hardening through his jeans. I couldn't think of anything better than to release it.

I reached down, and unzipped his pants while we continued to kiss. Once his dick was free I stroked the shaft. He palmed my face with both hands and kissed me more intensely as I worked on his stiff piece. I wanted to suck it. I wanted it in my mouth at that very second. I pulled my face away from his and stared at him. Neither of us said a word. He backed up toward the bed while removing his pants and shirt. I followed suit and removed my dress.

Once he sat down on the bed I got down on my knees and quickly stuffed his dick in my mouth. The taste was delicious. He was blessed with a dick that was long and thick so I stretched my mouth wide to fit it inside. With my deep throating skills, I could get all of it down past my tonsils. Each time he held on to the back of my head and moaned loudly. That excited me, only making for a more intense blowjob. I would only come up for air when I thought he was nearing an eruption. I wasn't trying to end the night that quickly.

"Babe, you gotta stop," he moaned.

I giggled a little before I stopped since I knew if he said stop, that meant, "I'm about to bust all in your mouth in a minute."

"Come here," he said, pulling me up from the floor.

He leaned back on the bed and pulled me up over his face. He began French kissing my clit. I almost came immediately. With his thick-ass lips and his strong tongue, I held it together for only a couple minutes before my body was trembling. He licked, and sucked me into five consecutive orgasms before pulling me down to sit on his dick.

It slid in with ease, and I went to work riding him like a trained horse jockey. My walls were filled with his warmth as he hit my G-spot continuously. Sweat was dripping off of me despite how cold the room was from the air conditioning. My body temperature had to be feverish. We continued until both of our bodies fell limp, and I rested on his chest before falling to sleep. I loved this man, and there wasn't any other person I'd rather be with.

Chapter Fourteen

Virginity

Desire

"Where are you taking me?" I asked with my hands stretched out in front of me.

"I told you that it was a surprise," he said as he held me by the hand, slowly guiding me.

At eighteen, the only surprises that I was used to weren't good ones. I never knew what was coming although I was prepared for anything. It was my birthday and, for once, I was looking forward to it. For once, I didn't have to worry about my mother forgetting or my sister trying to convince me that she didn't buy my card and sign our mother's name. I would've never expected Dontay to be so thoughtful and caring. From what you heard on the street, you'd have thought he was the meanest and nastiest person on earth. I'd been privileged to see a different side of him and, for me, it was a blessing.

"Please, just give me a little hint?" I whined. I knew he wouldn't tell me, but it was worth a try.

"We're almost there, just chill. I told you that patience is a virtue. Good things come to those who wait. I know that you've heard that one before," he said. I heard the sound of music. I tried to listen to see if I could figure it out, but no such luck.

"Almost there. Just a few more steps," he said before stopping and standing in front of me.

A few seconds later he removed the blindfold that I had been wearing. I'd hoped that it didn't mess up my eye makeup and have me standing there looking like a raccoon. In front of me were hundreds of roses, literally. I had never seen so many roses in one place in my life. There were huge bouquets everywhere. Pink and white with an amazing aroma.

"What is this?" I was shocked. I didn't even know what to say. For once, I was speechless. I had never seen a sight so breathtaking.

"It's your birthday. I wanted to show you how special you are," he said.

I looked around the room. I didn't even know where we were. There was a table in the center of the room that sat on top of rose petals. There were candles on either side of a runner that led to the table. Even on TV I'd never seen anything like it.

"Come on," he said, grabbing me by the hand and leading me toward the table.

He pulled out my chair for me and kissed me on the cheek as he pushed me up to the table. Was I dreaming? Because I never wanted to wake up if so. He sat down on the opposite side of the table.

"I can't believe that you did all this for me," I said. We hadn't even had sex yet. I thought for sure he would have pressured me into it a very long time ago. I could probably bet on the fact that he'd been sleeping with other women in the meantime. I was just surprised that he was still around. A man in a bow tie appeared carrying a large silver platter with a lid. Dontay nodded at the man who removed the lid. I was expecting dinner to be underneath. A nice steak or some sort of chicken, but there sat a small blue box. The man leaned over to allow me to retrieve it. I was almost afraid of what I would find.

"Open it," he said.

I took a deep breath before I opened it. Sitting there was the biggest diamond I'd ever seen up close. "What is this?" I asked.

"It's a promise ring," he said with a smile. He could probably sense how nervous I was. I probably would've passed out if he'd asked me to marry him. I certainly wasn't ready for that.

"What is the promise?"

"That I will never leave you, and that I will never hurt you. I've never felt this way about any other woman. Even though we haven't been intimate, I feel like we have an unbreakable connection. Something that no one could tear apart."

"You never cease to amaze me, you know that? Every time I think that things couldn't get any better, they do. I never want to know what it feels like to be without you so I will accept this promise ring. I will also promise you the same. Now put it on me," I demanded.

Even though it wasn't an engagement ring, I still wanted him to place it on my finger. He reached across the table and slowly placed it on my ring finger.

"Thank you. I really appreciate this. It's beautiful."

"There's more where that came from," he said just as the guy in the tux appeared again.

Just like before, he had a silver platter in his hand. This time, the box was a long, slim box. I grabbed it and this time there was a diamond bracelet inside. The diamonds were flawless, shining and glistening with even the slightest movement. I didn't even have a chance to put it on before the man returned once again with a smaller box. I opened that one to find a key ring with two keys.

"What are these to?" I asked, confused.

"One is to my house, and the other is to your new car."

"What?" I screamed.

He just laughed at my excitement. He'd truly outdone himself. It didn't even matter to me what type of car it was. I would've been happy with a Honda at that point. I wanted to be with him forever. I truly didn't want this to end. After the gift giving was through, the man returned with our food.

"You're beautiful, you know that?" he said as he watched me intently.

I was blushing so hard I was sure that my cheeks were red. I could tell that he was sincere. I hadn't done anything extra, nothing over the top. I was just myself. Growing up, not many boys looked my way. Even though to some I was drop-dead gorgeous, to some I was hideous. Being of mixed race, there was always a few people who looked at you sideways.

As time went on, we were closer than close; that is, until I found out about his relationship. My sister always warned me about men like him. She told me that they almost always had someone. I didn't believe her and because of that, I felt like a damn fool. I went so far as to follow him to watch what was happening before I approached him with it. I wanted to be sure. I wanted proof before bringing it up. Once I had gathered everything, I let him have it. Told him that I was walking away forever. What I didn't realize was that in the game of love forever doesn't last forever. Our hearts are very unpredictable.

I tried to keep my distance from him. I even tried to give his ring back, but he wouldn't take it. It wasn't until a year later that an awkward situation landed me in his arms again. I was having a birthday party, and I decided to give this club a try, not knowing that he was actually one of the owners. I called and left a message regarding my ideas and waited for someone to call me. I got a call later that day and was told to come down. I was shocked when I walked in to make all of the arrangements to find him sitting behind the desk. I almost turned around and walked out.

"Desire, wait! I have something to ask you."

"What's that?" I asked, letting the handle of the door loose from my grip.

"Do you ever think about what life would be like if you and I would have stayed together instead of me dealing with Tracy?"

"I think about it all of the time, but it doesn't matter now that I know she's your wife."

"It does matter. You know how I felt about you then and not much has changed."

"I would find that really hard to believe. When I was just ready to give us a try, you were already with her."

"I didn't think that you wanted to be with me," he said, moving closer to me.

"I wanted you, and I thought that you would have figured it out."

"I guess I was blind then. My eyes weren't open, but they are wide open now." He grabbed my hand, and I tried to resist. I could feel the heat from his body as he moved closer to me. I wanted to turn around and run out of the door, but I couldn't. I loved this man once, and I knew that it had never died. I had morals, and I knew that it was definitely wrong to yearn for another woman's husband. I backed away a little when he moved his lips close to mine.

"What are you doing, Dontay?" I quizzed him as I backed up even closer toward the exit.

"I miss you, Desire," he said, wrapping his arms around me.

"Dontay, this isn't right. Please don't," I said as I continued to weakly try to push him away.

"You know that you can't resist me. You want me just as bad as I want you."

"That's not true, I . . ." I said before his lips touched mine. He stopped me in midsentence. I didn't want to move forward, but it felt too good to back away anymore. His lips touching mine brought back all of the memories that I tried to put behind me.

He held on to me tight, and I let his initiated motion finish through completely. As he began to rub his hands across my back, I felt myself getting wet down below. He slowly hiked up my miniskirt and pulled my panties down with ease. He hadn't even touched my throbbing hot spot yet, but I was already nearing an orgasm from the way that he flickered his tongue around my neck. I let out a little moan once his fingers finally made their way to my tunnel. He lifted me up onto the table with his fingers still inserted. He moved his fingers in and out slowly causing my juices to cover his two digits completely. I nibbled on his ear as he continued using his fingers to satisfy me. I was about to burst and tried not to scream as the climax forced me to hold on to him tightly. I could hear voices outside and as the sounds grew closer I lost my focal point.

"Dontay, stop. I think Tracy's coming," I said, pushing him away.

"What?"

"I hear her voice. Shit, Dontay, where can I hide?" I said, fumbling to straighten my clothing.

"Go into the men's room. She won't come in there," he said, now realizing that it was in fact her coming close to the door. As she opened the door, he turned and greeted her. I watched from a crack in the bathroom door.

"Hey, baby, what are you doing here?" he said, trying with his foot to cover my thong that was still lying on the floor.

"Tanya and I were going to the mall. I missed you so I just wanted to stop by and tell you."

"You could have called me on the phone and told me that."

"Well, I wanted to tell you face to face and, anyway, whose car is that outside?"

"Oh, that's really why you came in. You saw a car and wanted to check on me. You ain't slick!"

"No, that's not what happened, but I would still like to know."

"Belongs to someone who came here to put down a deposit on a party."

"Oh, really? Well, where are they? Why is the car still outside? And I can tell it belongs to a female. I'm not stupid, you know," she said loudly.

"Yeah, it does belong to a female. She came to drop off the money, and her car wouldn't start. She called some dude to come get her," he responded with a straight face.

"Really?" she quizzed him, obviously still not convinced. "Well, I'm on my way to the mall. I'll see you later at home," she said before kissing him good-bye and heading toward the door.

Dontay followed and locked the door behind her. "You can come out now!" he yelled through the club.

"Damn, Dontay, that shit was too close. This shit cannot go on. Let's just forget that today ever happened!"

"I can't forget. I need you, Desire, and that's some real shit. I've fucked with plenty of women but none give me the feeling that you do."

"Dontay, save it. If you wanted me, you would've never lied to me about being married. Look, I have to go. I'm going to forget this, and I would suggest that you do the same!" I quickly walked out of the club and entered my car. I drove away with a nervous feeling in my gut. I knew how I felt about him, and I also knew that there was no way I would ever forget what'd just happened. I was going to attempt to move on with life without him regardless of how difficult that would be. We never realize how difficult temptation is to avoid until we are staring it in the face.

A few weeks following the incident at the club I was doing some shopping at the Gallery shopping mall in downtown Philadelphia. Retail therapy was always something that would make me feel just a little bit better when I wasn't in the best mood. I'd picked up a few new handbags and a couple pairs of shoes and was on my way to the parking lot when I heard someone call my name. The voice was all too familiar. It was Dontay. I turned back around with a frown and walk toward my car. A good day had just been ruined.

"Look, can we talk?" he asked, slowly driving beside me as I continued to walk.

"Talk about what, Dontay?"

"About us. Listen, I just need a few minutes of your time, and if you never want to talk to me again after that, I will respect your decision."

I continued walking without speaking. All sorts of thoughts were going through my mind. I wanted to tell him to fuck off, but I loved him. I'd never expected things to turn out the way that they had since I believed his every word. I believed him when he told me he loved me and he would make things right. Most people would think I was crazy, and they'd probably be right in that assumption. I was crazy—crazy in love.

"Just follow me to my house," I said before getting in the car and shutting the door.

He followed me to my house and the few minutes of talking quickly turned into a few minutes of touching followed by a few minutes of fucking. I let my feelings for him take over, and I gave in. I couldn't resist anymore and though I felt guilty afterward, I wasn't guilty enough to leave him alone. I knew that he would never be mine, but I imagined it each time we were together.

After he left, I hurried to get dressed and make it to Zanzibar Blue just in time for our girly dinner. It took me three circles around the block to find a parking lot that I was willing to park my BMW in. I wasn't about to put that shit into a valet lot so that some asshole could put a dent in it. Though I had an okay job, this car was a gift, and I wasn't ready to pay for any damages, especially ones that I didn't cause. After comfortably self-parking, I began the two-block walk to the restaurant. I was greeted by the hostess and escorted to the table where my girls Cindy and Gina were waiting.

"Hey, girls, what's up?" I said before hugging them both. "Damn I thought I was going to be the last one here. Where are Octavia and Shany?"

"I don't know. Octavia is probably trying to pry Shany away from that husband of hers," Cindy said with a chuckle.

"Yeah, they have been spending a lot of time together. I guess they've kissed and made up now," Gina spoke before taking a sip of water.

"Well, I wish they would hurry up, because I'm hungry as hell," I said, rubbing my growling stomach.

"Those niggas can buy you cars, but they can't feed your ass, huh?" Cindy said, laughing.

"Fuck you, Cindy! I can get them to buy me anything I want. Don't get it twisted!" I said, snapping my fingers like the gay skit on *In Living Color*.

"I'm just playing, girl!" she said, tapping her hands on the table and laughing loudly.

"Hey, ladies, sorry I'm late. My man was all over me and shit!" Shany said as she walked up to the table from behind.

"Where's Octavia?" Cindy quizzed her.

"Oh she couldn't make it. Some bullshit about a babysitter. I think she lied to go see that married man she's been messing around with," Shany spoke before sitting down.

"So what's up with you and him? I guess you've kissed and made up now huh?" Gina asked, smiling. I sat there burning inside because I was surely not interested in her reply.

"We did. He told me that he hasn't cheated on me, and I have to believe him. I know that he loves me, and I know that it ain't a bitch out there who can compare to me. I dropped it, and I promised him that I wouldn't bring it up again. Then he tore my back out if you know what I mean!" She began laughing at her insinuation of good sex.

I sat there close to vomiting. I knew that I was about to lose it so I quickly excused myself from the table to go to the restroom. I wanted to scream as I stood in front of the mirror. I couldn't sit and listen to stories of their happiness when I was unhappy in my own life. As bad as it may sound, I was happy when they weren't. Nobody wants to hear stories about other people being happy when they are miserable.

After I got myself together I returned to the table after about ten minutes with a blank stare on my face. I was hoping that no one would notice since none of them even came and checked to see if I was okay after being away from the table so long.

"What's wrong with you?" Shany asked, noticing my change in appearance.

"I don't feel well all of a sudden. I think I'm going to head home and lie down," I said after grabbing my bag.

"Okay, well, call later and let us know how you feel," Cindy spoke.

"I will," I said as I made my way out of the restaurant. I was disgusted. I couldn't sit at the table with her any longer. I had been friends with Shany for over ten years but, after a while, I felt like she no longer supported me and that changed the way I felt about her completely. There was a time when she was my only friend, but once she got married she forgot all about me. She literally left me out to dry. While I watched her relationship grow I couldn't help but be envious. That should've been my life. That fact made it hard for me to be the great friend I once was. I knew that most people would say that I was wrong, but I didn't give a damn.

Once I made it home, I immediately called Dontay. I wasn't happy about the way things left off when I last saw him at the club. I was getting more distressed the longer I sat and thought about it. I'd let it sit on my heart long enough, and it was about time I spoke about it. I dialed his cell phone, and once he answered it, I began to yell immediately.

"I can't believe you! Why would you do that to me knowing that she was on her way?" I yelled into the receiver.

"First of all, I didn't know she was coming—and what the fuck is your problem?"

"My problem is the bullshit games that you continue to play. You told me that you loved me, you promised that you wouldn't hurt me, yet you continue to pull me back in just to be hurt!"

"I never said anything changed. I never said that you and I would be together."

"Fuck this, Dontay! I thought that things were going to change. I thought that you wanted me to be happy."

"I do want you to be happy, but you know the dilemma I'm faced with here. I'm not sure what to do, and you aren't making the decision any easier for me. All I am asking for is a little time."

"I'm done with this conversation, Dontay, and you. Good-bye!" I said before ending the call. He called me and left at least five messages. How did I get myself into this? I wondered what was going on with me mentally that I continued to fall in love with him. I wanted to be in a real relationship for once in my life, but the drug dealers and other big timers I was attracted to only did me dirty each time. I was tired of being number two. I thought that I would be satisfied with the jump off title, but I was ready to be wifey. I thought that the more time I spent with Dontay the more he would love me and the more likely he would be to leave Tracy's ass alone.

I lay on the bed for about an hour, sulking in my own misery, when I heard the doorbell ring. I wasn't quick to answer it, since I figured it was the girls checking to see how I was doing, and I was definitely not in the mood for a get-well session. After about five rings, I was annoyed, so I got up to go answer it. I peeked out of the peephole and noticed Dontay standing there impatiently. *What the hell does he want?* I thought before answering it. I contemplated leaving him standing there and going back up to bed, but I knew how persistent he was, and I figured that he wouldn't leave me alone no matter what, and it would be tough to get rid of him.

"What the hell do you want?" I asked through a small crack in the door.

"I want to talk. Open the door, Desire," Dontay said, trying to push the door open.

"I don't have anything to say, and I don't feel really well so I need to get back to bed," I said, attempting to close the small space between us.

"Look, just give me five minutes. That's all I'm asking for. I need to explain some things to you."

I thought about turning him away, but my feelings for him were overriding my anger. As he stood there looking pitiful, I warmed up inside, because my heart still yearned for his attention. "Five minutes, that's it!" I spoke sternly before loosening my grip on the door to allow him to enter the house.

"Look, I didn't mean to shut you out earlier, but I was a little upset that you called me yelling. I know that I was wrong to lie to you about her. It's a lot harder than I thought it was going to be to walk away from her. I know that I should have been honest with you and told you that things between me and her were going okay, but I'm sorry if I led you on."

"So what does that mean, you don't want to deal with me anymore?"

"I didn't say that I didn't want you. I'm saying that I'm confused. I care for you and her, and it's hard for me to make a choice."

"I can't wait around forever, Dontay. I either need you to be with me or leave me alone so that I can move on with my life."

"I can't do that," he spoke before moving closer to me. I pushed him away trying to avoid any physical contact. I was hurting, and I was still angry about the way that he dragged me along.

"Stop it, Dontay. I know what you are trying to do, and it's not going to work." I backed away as I usually did when I was angry with him.

"I need you, Desire," he said, wrapping his arms around my waist and beginning to caress the small of my back. I tried to stand firm and push him away, but I needed him as much as he claimed he needed me. I felt like the biggest sucker for falling for his tricks, but he had me right where he wanted me. He softly placed a kiss on my lips that sent chills through my body. He pushed his tongue through my lips and began to massage mine with his. It was as if all of my anger was being completely drained from my body and refilled with love.

My body was warm and my feet were tingling. I quickly forgot about Mrs. Tracy as he was my man again, if only for a short time to make love to me. As his hands made their way to my panties, I became excited, anticipating him touching my wetness. "I'll never stop wanting you," he whispered in my ear causing me to exude an overload of lubrication.

After meeting my clit with his soft touch, I moved my hips to initiate a circular motion. This man was all that I could ever ask for, minus the wife. I wanted to feel him inside of me and his fingers caressing me were causing me to hunger for more. "I'm going to make you mine, I promise," he whispered before lifting me up to place me on the sofa. I unzipped his pants as he continued to finger fuck me with ease. I was moaning loudly, and he was growing harder with each sound I made. I pulled his manhood out and stroked it with a tight grip not ever wanting to let it go. I rubbed his length and begged him to get inside of me. "You want me to fuck you?" he asked in a low tone.

"Yes!" I moaned.

"I don't believe you. Tell me again," he instructed while moving his fingers in and out a little faster.

"Yes!" I moaned a second time.

"I still don't believe you. I need you to make me believe it," he instructed.

"Fuck me please, Dontay. I need this dick inside of me!" I moaned loudly.

With that he freed his fingers from my extremely juicy tunnel and rammed his stick inside of me. I was in ecstasy as he worked in slow, steady strokes that exuded force. He continued his stroke while sticking his tongue in and out of my mouth. I yelled as I climaxed, and he picked up speed when he noticed my body starting to tremble. He soon turned me over and smacked my ass a few times. I loved it, and when he asked me whose pussy it was, I didn't hesitate to scream his name. It did belong to him, and he knew that no matter what I would always return to him. I sat there looking into his eyes as he pumped harder trying to satisfy me. Oh, I loved this man, and I whispered it into his ear continuously as he hit my G-spot time and time again. He then removed his length from my wetness and quickly shoved it into my ass. I was used to this since I had learned early on that this was one way to satisfy him. He loved a woman who could take it in the ass and that was one thing that Tracy had yet to tolerate. He always called me his little soldier, because even from the first time he tried it, I always acted as if I enjoyed it. He moved in and out of my ass as I stuck two fingers inside of my tunnel to initiate another orgasm. I was nearing another climax when the telephone started to ring. I was focused on one more nut so I couldn't have cared less about who was calling. Once the answering machine picked up I tried even harder to ignore it, but Dontay seemed to be slowing down as he heard the answering machine come on. Maybe the sound of the beep made him realize he was making a mistake. Was I the mistake or was his wife? Either way, something made him slow down. After a few more seconds, he stopped and sat down on the sofa before placing his face in his hands. "What the fuck am I doing?" he yelled.

"Look, Desire, I have to go. I'll call you later," he said, fumbling to gather his clothing.

"What?" I quizzed both confused and annoyed. I knew that I shouldn't have let his ass in! "Where are you going?" I asked as I stood up from the sofa.

"I have to get home before she does or she'll wonder where I was," he said, zipping his pants.

"Why? Tell her you are working. You can't leave me hanging like that, Dontay," I said, grabbing hold of his hand trying to get him to refocus on me.

"I'm sorry, Desire, but I have to go. I'll give you a call tomorrow I promise."

I released my grip as he turned to walk out of the door. I wanted to beg him to stay, but I knew it would only make things worse. He couldn't live without me, but it was becoming clear that he couldn't live without her either.

Chapter Fifteen

Anniversary

Tracy

Here I was in the hospital staring at the ceiling while my husband was out doing God knows what with God knows who. I was in a lot of pain, but I refused all pain medication since I had nothing left to remember my baby. At least I could hold on to that. At five months pregnant, I had lost our first child, and he wasn't even around to comfort me. I could partly blame him for it, since I was constantly stressed with all of the drama he put me through, but I blamed myself. I should have been strong enough to walk away, if not for myself, then for the baby. Now I had nothing left but an empty womb and a busy signal every time I dialed Dontay's phone.

It was hours before I was actually able to reach him, and I was sure he felt like the biggest asshole in the world when he found out what happened. He came to the hospital and entered the room putting on an act that deserved an Academy Award.

"Baby, I got here as fast as I could. I am so sorry I wasn't here for you. How did this happen?" he asked while rubbing my forehead.

"I really don't want to talk about it right now. I'm in a lot of pain, and I really just want to go to sleep."

"Baby, I need to know what happened."

"Well, maybe if you weren't out fucking around on me you would have been here to know. I just lost our baby and that is the most pain I've ever been through. Right now I don't want to talk and that's that!" I responded, before turning away from him.

"Baby?"

"Dontay, please just let me sleep."

"Well, if it means anything to you, I wasn't out fucking around. I was actually working this time."

Instead of responding I let a tear fall from my eye. *This time!* As if one time was enough to erase the previous times he cheated.

From the outside looking in you would believe that we were the happiest couple in the world, but we were both pretty good at acting, and it had been enough to convince everyone that things were perfect. Dontay had mastered faking his love for me, and I had mastered faking as if it didn't matter. In all actuality it did matter, and I hoped that from this point on we could work at getting the old feelings back.

Once I was released from the hospital, Dontay played the perfect husband, but all good things must come to an end, and I knew that it wouldn't be long before things went back to normal.

It was the day before our anniversary and since neither of us could take off work the following day I planned to cook dinner and spend some quality time with Dontay, which was something that we hadn't done in a long time. I prepared a salmon and rice bake, with steamed vegetables, and topped it off with white wine. I got dressed in a little black dress that was sure to turn him on and after setting the table I sat down and waited for him to come in. After two hours of waiting, I dialed his cell phone. He answered on the first ring.

"Hello."

"Dontay, where are you?" I asked, annoyed.

"I'm working, why?"

"Why? Because our anniversary is tomorrow, and I told you that I had something special planned tonight!"

"Oh, shit, baby, it slipped my mind. I got backed up at worked, and I had some things to finish."

"Well, what time will you be home?" I asked, hoping that he would be here soon.

"Umm, I'm not sure. I still have a lot to do."

"Dontay, I went through a lot of trouble to make tonight special for you. Why can't you cut things short and finish up tomorrow? And why are you at work anyway? I thought you were going to the gym."

"I did go to the gym, but I got a call from work, and I needed to come finish some things up. Look, I'll try to get there as soon as I can."

"You know what, Dontay? Don't even bother! If our anniversary isn't important to you then why should it be to me?" Click.

I hung up the phone, and in a rage, I threw everything that I had cooked into the trash. Never mind the fact that I had spent over one hundred dollars getting everything together and slaved over the stove for hours.

I was pissed that after all of the time we'd been married, he couldn't even take one day off of cheating to spend it with me. I knew that his story about work was bullshit since he never worked on Sundays. I wasn't even going to fight him about it. Instead I took off my clothes and headed up to bed. Unfortunately, his cold hands touching my face at one o'clock in the morning awakened me.

"What?" I yelled, aggravated.

"I bought something for you!"

"Our anniversary is tomorrow, Dontay!"

"Actually it's one o'clock so it's okay for you to open it," he responded, reminding me of the fact that he'd been out all night.

"Well, I'm tired and I have to get up to go to work early in the morning, so it's going to have to wait until then!" I yelled, ignoring the fact that he was practically shoving the box in my face.

"Okay, no problem. It will be waiting here when you get up."

I turned over and headed back to sleep. I never felt him climb into bed that night, but I figured that he was most likely angry that I didn't open his gift. The alarm clock went off at six, which startled me since I usually set it for seven. *How the hell did the time get changed?* I thought as I pushed the off button. I sat up on the edge of the bed and rubbed my eyes before opening them. I couldn't believe my eyes. There were roses placed all around the room with a big HAPPY ANNIVERSARY banner in front of them. *How the hell did he manage to get this in here?* I walked over to the small table that displayed a purple jewelry box. I opened it to reveal a ring with five diamonds placed in a platinum setting. A tear fell as I began to feel bad about accusing him of cheating. Here he was out trying to make things right for me, and I thought something altogether different. The roses were beautiful, and I rushed out of the bedroom and as I looked down I noticed rose petals leading to the direction of the stairs. I followed the trail and as I got closer to the kitchen I could smell the scent of breakfast. I walked in and smiled as he stood over the table placing sausage and eggs on the plates.

"Baby, I can't believe you!" I said as I greeted him with a kiss.

"Happy anniversary, baby." He smiled.

"I'm sorry for snapping on you last night. I—"

"Don't worry about it. I totally understand, but I wanted to do something special for you, and it took me a little more time than I expected."

"Would you mind if I had this breakfast to go?"

"To go? Why? I set the alarm clock early."

I didn't speak as I slid my hand into his boxers and massaged his length. I stuck out my tongue to lick his neck as he leaned his head to the side to enjoy it. His skin tasted of honey, and I realized how much I'd missed it as I took in the flavor. I rubbed my hands over his pole and once he was aroused I wrapped my hands around it and began to stroke it unhurriedly. I wanted to feel him inside of me, but I wanted to take my time and enjoy it. I felt that my man was deserving of satisfaction since he'd gone overboard to make our anniversary exceptional. Easing down on my knees, I began to plant wet kisses on the tip of his pulsing manhood, the thickness of my lips causing him to sigh. I savored the taste of his prerelease while watching him fight to keep his composure. Soon the head was meeting my tonsils with my hands cupping his jewels.

"Baby, you're killing me," he moaned, as I released him from my mouth long enough to instruct him to keep quiet. After he was satisfied, he bent me over the counter with my ass high in the air.

"Go ahead and slap it. You know I love that shit!" I instructed, loudly, and he didn't hesitate to oblige. After using his fingers to guide him inside of me, he began to moved in slow circles until I was extremely wet. I could feel the juices pouring out of me as he reached his hands around my waist to fondle my clit while still digging deep inside of me. I wanted him to pick up the pace and once I started pushing my ass back a little faster he got the point. Grabbing hold of my hips he pushed harder and deeper causing one orgasm after another. My legs were shaking, and I wasn't sure how much I could take. I bit my bottom lip awaiting his explosion. Soon he was bursting with pleasure and the warm feeling inside of my confirmed that he was satisfied.

"Could you wrap that food up for me, baby? I'm going to go hop in the shower!" I smiled and planted a wet kiss on his lips.

"No problem," he said while watching me walk away.

I hopped in the shower and headed off to work with the biggest smile on my face. I couldn't stop thinking about Dontay all day.

Chapter Sixteen

Another Round

Alisha

2006

"What time is the appointment with the planner?" Hope asked.

We weren't waiting a year to get married like most couples did. That was one of Desi's best qualities: he saw what he wanted and grabbed it. Two months had passed since his proposal, and the ceremony date was fast approaching. Four months was hardly enough time to plan a wedding, but with his money and my connections, we were making it happen.

"She said she was coming at six. What time is it now?"

I was trying to make sure that I had all my ideas lined up to present to her. I needed my wedding day to be perfect. I'd created a presentation board full of all the details. It was my inner Virgo that kept me highly organized, especially when it came to event planning.

"It's five forty-five now. I still can't believe you're getting married. Never thought I'd see the day."

"Shit, me either, but I'm embracing it. Desi is perfect for me."

"Yeah, he's crazy, and so are you. Match made in heaven." She laughed. "So what's up with that nigga Jay? He still stalking you?"

"Girl, no. Thank God. I was sick of him. Like seriously, you're mad because I took your money, but it's not like he ain't get shit in return. I laid up wit' him and his little-ass dick for months."

Hope laughed hysterically.

"I'm glad you can find the humor in that shit. I get sick every time I think about it. Last time I saw him he told me I was going to pay for doing him dirty. Girl, fuck him. Ain't nobody got time for that."

"You better watch your back, because that fool is crazy."

"Well, I'm psycho. Besides, with Desi by my side, I don't have to watch my back. He's got that under control." I laughed.

"Yeah, Desi ain't having that," she agreed.

The doorbell rang and a huge smile came across my face. I ran toward the door to let in Lisa, the wedding planner. "Sorry I'm a few minutes late. Traffic was insane," she said, stepping into the foyer and hugging me.

"It's no problem. I'm just glad you made it." I motioned with my hand to show her where I had my presentation set up.

She walked past me and into the house. She was impeccably dressed from head to toe. Nothing was out of place, and her makeup was flawless. She had some of the most expensive designer attire around. Her shoes alone would set you back three stacks. Hope stood and greeted her once we entered the living room.

"As you can see, I have a full presentation here for you." I smiled and walked over to the board that I had covered with a large piece of fabric. I wanted to reveal each piece separately as not to overwhelm her.

"I see. I'm ready when you are." She took a seat and removed a leather notebook case from her briefcase.

"Okay, well, first let me say there is no budget. My man wants me to be happy, and told me to buy whatever I want."

"My kind of man," Lisa replied.

"Yes, that's why I'm marrying him." I laughed. "So first, I love white so there is a ton of white in my idea. Since the venue is a large art gallery, we have tons of space to work with. I want the wedding indoors with the pre-reception portion in the foyer of the building. The actual reception will take place outside in the garden. Since it will happen in the evening, I'd like it to look like there are stars over the entire seated area."

"Okay, I see where you're going. Basically with a lighting effect that could be done," she replied.

"Yes, that's what I was thinking as well. Next . . ." I revealed the presentation board. "This is all of the must-haves. The flowers, floor runners—it's all here. I'd also like a video to be shown via their ceiling projector onto the walls of the gallery. I will have that video for you within the next few weeks."

"I have to say, you are one of the most organized brides I've ever met." She laughed.

I finished my presentation, which lasted about an hour. Afterward, we set up our next meeting and then she was on her way.

"Girl, you are going to kill his pockets, literally," Hope said as I reentered the living room.

"Well, he has plenty of money. He can afford it."

The doorbell rang again. I figured Lisa must've forgotten something so I immediately opened it without peeking through the peephole.

"Long time no see," Jay said, holding a gun in his right hand.

I immediately tried to shut the door, but he kicked it with his right foot and knocked me to the floor.

"Hope, run," I yelled.

"What the hell is . . ." She stopped in her tracks when she noticed Jay standing over me with the gun pointed at my head.

"If you run, I'll blow her fucking brains out," he said in a tone sharp enough to pierce your skin.

Hope immediately began to cry. I held it together as much as I could. He grabbed me by the hair, pulled me up from the floor, and pushed me into the living room where he forced both of us to sit down on the sofa. He sat down on the sofa opposite us and put his feet up on the edge of the coffee table.

"So, what do we have here? Someone is getting married, I see." He looked over at the presentation board.

Both of us remained quiet. I wasn't sure how to answer that question for fear that anything I said would anger him further.

"Cat got your tongue? Not Miss Mouth All Fucking Mighty. I asked a fucking question!" he yelled.

"It's me. I'm getting married," Hope blurted out.

"Bullshit, I see that big-ass rock on her finger. That's real noble of you to try to take up for your sister, but that shit will get you both killed."

"What do you want, Jay?" I asked. "Is it your money? I can get it all back to you."

"Fuck your money, bitch! You fucked with my mind and my heart. It ain't enough money in the world that can fix that shit."

"I never meant to hurt you, Jay. That's the truth," I pleaded.

"You don't know the meaning of that word. You made a nigga believe you loved me. You know how that shit feels to find out that it was a big-ass scam? Keep your ass still before I shoot your ass," he yelled noticing Hope inching over to her purse. "Now back to my question." He redirected his attention back to me.

"I don't know how it feels, but what I do know is that it wasn't intentional."

In the brief few seconds that his attention was on Hope I had pressed the silent alarm on my wrist. Desi was so worried that someone would try to harm me that he had this watch custom made that notified him immediately if I hit it. I was confident that he'd be there soon to get us out of this. I needed to stay on Jay's good side, and hold him off as long as possible.

"I'm really sorry, Jay. I really cared for you."

He sat there silent for a few seconds. "Why are you marrying this nigga? You know you should be with me."

I was stuck. I didn't know what to say in response to that. If I didn't agree, he'd be pissed. If I did, he might call me a liar and still be pissed. At this point, there wasn't anything that I could say or do to make him believe me. I was a good liar, but an angry person can often see right through lies.

"What can I do to make it up to you?"

"What can you do?" he asked, rubbing his temple. He probably didn't expect that question.

"Yes," I replied calmly. I didn't want him to sense my fear. I wanted him to believe in the words that were coming out of my mouth. I was silently praying that Desi would walk in any minute.

"Come here," he said, waving in his direction with the gun still firmly gripped in his right hand.

I didn't hesitate. I did as I was told. Hope grabbed a hold of my hand as I began to walk away.

"Didn't I tell your ass to sit still?" Jay walked briskly over to Hope and put the gun to her right temple. Tears began to flow freely from her eyes. Hope, unlike me, was a very emotional person. She'd always been. I was pretty much emotionless. The only time you would know what I was feeling was when I was angry. When I was pissed, there would be no question mark.

"Hey, baby, she's sorry. Let's go over here to the sofa," I said, placing my hand on his shoulder.

He looked at me, and shot me a devilish grin. He licked his lips, and removed the gun from its resting place. "A'ight," he agreed.

I exhaled. I couldn't bear living if anything happened to her. She was all the family I had left. It was then that I thought about the mistake that I made in dealing with him. There were numerous people who warned me about him, including his ex, but I always thought she was hating. I figured that she was still in love with him and trying to get rid of me to get him back.

Jay sat down on the sofa, and patted the cushion next to him for me to sit. I sat down and waited for further instruction. I looked over at Hope and saw her eyes widen. I wasn't sure what contributed to the shift in her facial expression, until I heard a loud bang and my ears began ringing. I looked at Jay's lifeless body slumped over to the right. I was completely covered in blood.

"Are you okay?" Desi said.

I'd never been happier to hear his voice. I jumped up from the sofa, and ran over to his open arms. I was so nervous that my entire body shivered and my teeth were chattering. I held on tight, afraid to let him go.

"I got you, babe. It's all over. I'm here," he whispered.

Even though I was confident that Desi would always have my back, at that moment I felt even more secure about becoming his wife.

Chapter Seventeen

Parking Lot Pimpin'

Desire

The night was beautiful. There was a perfect breeze blowing as Dontay and I walked hand in hand along Penn's Landing. The night was pretty quiet. For the first time, I was able to walk with my man in public. I was patient, just as he'd asked me to be, and now I was ready to reap the benefits. I'd found out about his relationship, and instead of walking away, I stayed to fight through it. I could've walked away, but what would I be left with? Even if I had to share him, it was better than the life that I would have without him.

"I'm so happy, Dontay, seriously," I said as I snuggled close to him.

"I'm glad to hear that. Just so you know, I'm happy too."

"I want to know more about you. You know I don't know that much about you."

"You know enough. I don't know what else there is that you want to know."

"Well, how did you get in the business? You've never told me that."

"Why do you want to know that?"

"Because I told you a lot about me."

"But I didn't ask you. There are parts of my past that I'd like to keep there. Besides, you haven't told me everything."

"Well, almost everything. It's still more than you've told me." I pouted. I hated the fact that we had secrets. For the past five months we'd been together almost every day and night, yet we did more fucking than anything else. Even when we spent quality time together, we barely talked. He always said it was his quiet time.

"Horse's older brother, that's how I got into the business," he said before sitting down on one of the benches that sat along the water. "Shit was tight around the house. My father stopped giving my mom money, and I got tired of watching her struggle. The end."

"Do you trust me, Dontay?"

"Of course I do. If I didn't trust you, I wouldn't be here."

"Well, if you trust me why won't you let me in? I feel like you have this wall up, and I don't know why."

"I mean why do we have to talk about this now? It's really fucking up a good night. What about the gunshot wound? You tell me about that, then I'll tell you more."

He knew how I felt about that. That was enough to put any conversation like this to an end. I just wasn't ready. That was a part of my past that I wish I could forget. Just to speak Tyrese's name filled my body with an uncontrollable pain. Before Dontay, that was the most important person to me. I wasn't ready, and I didn't see me being ready anytime soon.

"I didn't think you would. Now could we not ruin the rest of the night with this?"

"Okay," I replied while looking out at the water. I couldn't be mad. He was right. How could I expect him to be 100 percent open with me when I wasn't prepared to do the same?

"Let's do something," I blurted out.

"What?" He turned to me.

"Come on and I'll show you," I said as I grabbed him by the hand and pulled him up off of the bench.

I knew that there was only one thing that could turn this night around: some mind-blowing spontaneous sex. I always felt the need to impress him. I never wanted him to feel that he could get something better from someone else. I didn't care if I had to get down under the table in a restaurant to suck his dick. I would do anything to satisfy him. I headed in the direction of the parking garage where he'd parked his car.

"Why are we going to the car? I'm not ready to go yet."

"We're going to the car, but we aren't leaving." I had a devilish smirk all across my face. I licked my lips to let him know what I had on my mind.

"Oh yeah?" he asked while rubbing his hands across his freshly cut beard.

Once we made it to the car he hit the keypad to unlock the doors and turn off the alarm. Once he attempted to open the door I pushed it shut.

"Baby, what are you doing?" he asked, turning around and leaning up against the car. I moved closer to him and stood in between his legs. I stared at him before kissing him. I was in heaven as our tongues intertwined. I was getting extremely wet as he rubbed his hands across my back. I backed away from him for a second and began to loosen the buttons of my blouse. He stared at me like I was a succulent piece of steak on a platter.

"I want you now," I whispered.

"A'ight, let's get in the car," he said, reaching for the door.

"No, I want you right here, right now," I said as I revealed my braless breasts.

"What if someone drives by?"

I walked up to him, grabbed his hand, and directed it up under my skirt. My pussy was practically dripping it was so wet. It didn't take long before his finger was inside of me. A moan escaped me as he leaned in and began to kiss my neck. I could hear cars driving through the parking lot, but soon I was deaf to the sounds around me. I was more turned on that I'd ever been. I didn't care if anyone saw us. Hell, they could stop and watch and I'd still act as if they weren't even there. To me, at that moment, we were the only ones in the world. He turned me around and boosted me up onto the hood of the car. He nudged me a little forcing me to lie down. With one swift motion he ripped off my thongs and buried his face deep inside my pussy. I almost came immediately after contact. His tongue was warm and wet. The long, slow licks caused my body to shiver. He continued to lick my clit and would occasionally pause to suck on it while slowly letting it slip from the grips of his lips. He stuck two fingers inside of me and made love to me with them. It didn't take long for me to climax, and I could feel him taking in the juices as they were released. I almost lost my concentration as a car drove by and slowed down to enjoy a quick glance of our lust. Damn, I needed that. After I came twice all over his face, he stood up, licked his lips while staring at me, and unzipped his pants to release his hardness, which was about to burst through his jeans. Once it was unconfined, he rubbed the head of it up and down my pussy lips causing more juices to flow.

"Fuck me, please," I begged because my body was yearning for him. He slowly slid inside of me, but stopping just as my walls wrapped around the head. I squeezed as tight as I could to grip his entire width. I moved my hips to massage the tip. I could feel it coming out and immediately sliding back inside. After he could no longer stand the teasing, he rammed it inside of me with force, just the way I loved it. He placed his hand on my shoulders to aid him in digging deeper inside of my tunnel.

"Dontay, oooh shit, Dontay," I called out. I wanted to reassure him that he was doing the job well. He gained more momentum but at the same time I could tell that he was slowing down. "Baby, don't slow down."

"I'm not ready cum yet," he said before pulling out. He bent down to kiss me before standing to pull me off of the car. "Come on and ride this dick," he said.

He got on the car in same position that I'd just been in. I took off my shoes, climbed on top, and got in a squatting position. I rose up and down a few times taking only the tip in before pushing it deep inside of me. He moaned as I worked in circles. I could hear the echo of my ass slapping up against his legs as I picked up speed. Cars continued to drive by, and I kept riding him as if they were invisible. I was anxious to reach that climax, and I couldn't care less who was watching. I continued bouncing up and down on his dick. As I neared an orgasm, I pushed down and moved in circles, grinding and hitting my G-spot.

"Oh shit, baby, Ahhhh yes, yes, I'm cumming," I screamed.

He grabbed hold of my ass and held on tight as his warm cum filled my insides. I bent down to kiss him.

"I can't believe you," he said. "Come on and let's get the fuck outta here before they call the cops on us."

I laughed as I got off of him, picked up my shoes, and jumped in the passenger seat. He shook his head as he got inside and turned the car on.

"You're a bad influence you know that?" he said with a smile.

"You love me though," I replied.

"You're right. I love you."

Chapter Eighteen

Clubbing

Desire

That night the line to get into the club was ridiculous. I was planning on shining tonight and going home with a baller. I walked into the club and greeted everyone while I made my way to VIP. I noticed Shany and the girls at the table in the back. I walked up to them unnoticed.

"What's up, bitches? Didn't expect to see me huh?" I said, smiling as I stood the end of the table.

"Hey, girl, I thought you had moved or something. Can't call anybody?" Shany said, smiling before standing to hug me.

"I know I've been pretty bad with that but tonight let's go get our party on!" I said before turning to go out to the dance floor.

I grabbed man after man and shook my ass all over them. I had drunk at least four apple martinis, and I was feeling toasty. I could feel Dontay's eyes glued to me as I made my rounds, trying to find the nigga with the most money. I wasn't about to fuck with any average Joe. After about an hour of dancing, I needed to go to the bathroom. I walked toward the restroom and felt a tap on my shoulder. I turned around, annoyed because I hated for someone to approach me that way.

"What!" I yelled.

"What are you trying to do with all of the dancing and shit, make me jealous?"

"Dontay, please. I'm just growing a bit tired of playing number two. I'm trying to snag me a man, since that's a title you're obviously not trying to fill," I yelled. "Don't forget your wife is in here, so I'm sure you wouldn't want her to walk up on us conversing."

"Fuck that! I'm not going to sit here and watch you all up on these niggas and ignore it. That's just disrespectful," he yelled.

"You have some nerve to talk about someone being disrespectful. You are the one cheating on your wife!" I retorted.

"Look, let's go into the office and talk, please," he said, grabbing me by the arm.

"Dontay, I came here to enjoy myself. I really don't have time for this right now."

"Please, I need to talk to you," he pleaded.

"This is not the time or the place for this conversation. I told you that we were through," I said as I noticed Shany walking in the direction of the bathroom.

"What's going on? Are you okay?" she quizzed us after noticing the looks on both of our faces.

"I'm fine. This guy out on the dance floor pissed me off. I was just trying to let Dontay know to keep an eye on him because he was pretty drunk," I lied.

"Well, I'll handle that for you, and if he gives you any more trouble let me know," Dontay said before walking in the direction of his office. I stood there for a second, contemplating whether I should follow him, but even if I wanted to, I would have to duck Shany.

"Girl, these guys are crazy when they get drunk. There should be limit on the amount of drinks that they can buy," Shany said, laughing.

"Most definitely! Well, I'll see you when you get back out to the floor," I said, cutting the conversation short. I began walking away as I waited for her to go into the restroom. Once I heard the door open and close I turned around and quickly made my way to Dontay's office. I knocked on the door, and he opened it within seconds.

"Thanks for coming to talk," he said as I entered the plush office.

"So what is it that you wanted to talk about?" I asked since I knew we didn't have much time to talk.

"I'm ready to leave her." He began to speak, and I began to tune him out, since I'd been hearing this same tune for the last two years. "I need someone like you in my corner. Tracy can't be who I want her to be. I just need you to trust me. Do you trust me?" he asked while staring at me and stroking my hand.

"Yes, I trust you," I said excitedly, since those were the words that I'd been longing to hear.

"Kiss me," he said as he moved closer. I sucked in the smell of his cologne and as I closed my eyes I imagined that we were somewhere else. I licked his lips as he began to fondle me. My mind was running in circles since I wasn't sure if he was playing me again. I had fallen for his tricks over and over again. I relaxed as he backed me up against the desk that was located in the center of the office. He kneeled down and slowly raised my leg over his shoulder. He moved my panties to the side and buried his face down below. The swift movements of his tongue against my clit caused my body to shiver.

I palmed the back of his hand to create more pressure before I exploded. He licked his lips as he stood up from the floor. He unzipped his pants and pulled his length through his boxers signaling me to go to work. I squatted just enough so that my mouth was at an even height with it. I grabbed a hold of it and slowly licked around the head to savor the taste of the pre-cum. A sigh escaped his lips as I allowed him to shove it into my mouth. I grabbed hold of his balls with my free hand and gently began to massage them at the same time. "You like that?" I quizzed him before deep throating him once more.

"Come on and let me fuck you!" he instructed. I rose up from the squatting position and turned around facing the desk. I put one leg up on the chair and waited for him to enter from behind. He grabbed hold on to my waist and used it to aid him in pumping harder. I screamed for him to go faster, and he sped up and added more force. I heard a faint knock at the door, but I didn't want to stop. I ignored it as I neared my next climax. The knock continued, but we were both so wrapped up in the moment that it didn't matter what else was going on around us.

The noises we were both making were getting louder as he and I both were enjoying it. After it was all over with, I went back out to enjoy the party even though I felt stupid. I didn't know what the hell I was doing or why. I had to figure things out ASAP because things were out of control.

Chapter Nineteen

Ruthless

Dontay

"I don't give a fuck who he's related to. That mutha-fucker stole from me, and I want his ass gone. Do you hear me?" I yelled.

I was furious. I couldn't stand a thief. I did way too much for niggas to steal from me, and I didn't appreciate that shit one bit. Darron was a young nigga I'd given a shot. I took him from the pissy-ass projects and put him up in a condo and this was the way that he decided to repay me. His runs were consistently coming up short. Over a month's time he'd stolen somewhere close to thirty grand. Thirty grand was small change, but it was the principle. You don't take from the hand that feeds you.

"When you find him, take him over to the warehouse and call me," I yelled.

"All right," Horse replied before hanging up.

I was furious. I didn't get this far by allowing shit to slip through the cracks. There was a knock on the door just as I got off the phone. "Come in."

"Desire is out front. You want me to let her in?" Jules said as he cracked open the door.

"Nah, not right now. Tell her I'm handling some shit right now and I'll stop by to see her later."

"She looks like she's upset about something."

"She always looks like that. Just tell her what I said."

"Got it," he said before closing the door.

I couldn't see Desire at that moment. I needed to focus on the situation at hand. About a minute later my cell phone began to ring. I knew it was her without even looking at the caller ID. I picked up.

"You really told him not to let me in? What you got a bitch back there?" she yelled.

"Naw, it ain't no bitch in here. I have a situation that I need to deal with. Now ain't the time."

"I have something important to talk to you about."

"It's gonna have to wait. Look this is Horse on the other line. I gotta take this. I'll see you later," I said before switching over.

"Got him."

"A'ight, I'm on my way."

I slipped out the back door avoiding Desire and hopped in the car. I was driving well over the speed limit on my way down to the warehouse. I planned to make an example out of him in the event any other nigga thought it was good idea to steal from me.

I made it to the warehouse and Horse was standing at the front waiting for me. I took off my jacket and passed it to him and continued walking inside. In the back of the warehouse two of the workers were standing next to Darron, who was tied up in a chair. He was slumped over in the chair asleep. There was blood on his shirt that had run from his nose.

"Wake his bitch ass up," I said as I rolled up my sleeves.

Rob slapped him on the side of his face a few times until he woke up.

"Aww, man, Dontay, it wasn't me, man, I swear. I would never steal from you."

"I guess you think I'm stupid right?"

"Nah, man, never," he pleaded.

I stood there putting on gloves. It didn't matter to me how much he cried. His fate was now in my hands. I reached over to Horse, who was holding a chainsaw in his hand.

"Please, Don, man, I'm begging you don't do this." He tried to wiggle his hands free from the cuffs. I was unfazed. I could remember it as if it were yesterday when I put him on. He reminded me of myself when I was his age. He was hungry and wanted to get his momma out of the hood. Just like me, his father wasn't in his life. Just like me, he had dreams and aspirations and those plans were derailed when he watched his mother work a minimum-wage job every day. Was I wrong for punishing him? I didn't think so, and honestly I didn't give a fuck what anyone thought. In this game, loyalty is a must and a slip up will get you fucked up. He didn't deserve to breathe the same air that I did. Instead of being patient and waiting his turn, he thought he could start up his own organization with my money.

I pulled the cord turning on the chainsaw and watched him quiver. I couldn't hear him over the noise. I was tired of the sound of his voice anyway. It was time to kiss his ass good-bye.

The first slice went through his chest. Blood shot everywhere. The plastic which covered the floor beneath him immediately was covered. Horse, Rob, and Tip backed away to avoid getting it all over their clothes. His body was shaking uncontrollably, but he was still alive. I wanted him to suffer. I wasn't going to make it that easy. I took another slice through his stomach. His eyes widened as he screamed in agony. I smiled. Yes, I smiled. It felt good, as sick as that may sound.

He was foaming at the mouth, blood spilled out. I could feel his blood running down my face. My hands were completely covered. I took a few swipes at his knees before taking the final cut to his neck, decapitating him. Rob turned around, I could tell he was sick to his stomach. Not everyone was built for this. When I was done, I looked like Carrie covered in the pigs' blood. I turned off the chainsaw and set it down on the ground. Horse was standing there with a stone face waiting for me to give orders. I stepped out of my shoes, socks, pants, and took off my shirt before stepping off the plastic. Horse passed me a towel to wipe off what blood I could without water. I walked to the front, barefoot in boxers. There were a pair of jeans, Air Force Ones, and a button-up folded. I put on the clothes and walked out to the car. Horse was behind me.

"You good?" I asked him as I sat down in the car with the door open.

"Yeah, I'm cool. You?"

"I'm good. We need to have a meeting tomorrow. Sometime in the afternoon, but I'll hit you up later on to confirm the details."

"All right. What you want me to do here?"

"Chop him up and throw him over the bridge," I said nonchalantly.

"All right," Horse said as he reached in the car to shake my hand.

I pulled the door closed and drove away. I needed to get a shower and see what the fuck was so important with Desire. I made it to her house twenty minutes later. All of the lights were on downstairs so I knew she was waiting on me. I opened the door and made my way toward the stairs. She called from the living room.

"Dontay?"

"Yeah," I said, taking a few steps. I wanted to get to the shower before she noticed the remnants of blood that still remained on my skin.

I heard her shoes on the hardwood floor making her way into the hallway. "We need to talk," she said with her arms folded.

"After I get a quick shower we can talk," I said, continuing up the stairs.

"Oh, so you want to try to wash that bitch's pussy juices off? Huh, Dontay? You aren't slick, you wouldn't let me in the office, now you're running to the shower. You know I'm not stupid. You tell me you aren't fucking her, yet your actions show something else. I'm sitting here like a dumb ass, being loyal to you with the hope that you'll be mine. How would you feel if I'd been out fucking another nigga?" she yelled.

I stopped in my tracks, turned around, and stormed back down the stairs. I walked over to her, close enough for her feel my breath. "Does this look like pussy juice to you?" I said, putting my hands in her face.

She backed up a few steps and looked down at my hands with wide eyes. She didn't say another word. She knew it was in her best interest not to.

"Now, like I said, we'll talk after I get out of the shower."

I turned and went upstairs to the master bedroom. After taking off the clothes that I was wearing, I jumped in the shower. I could hear her enter the bathroom and leave again. I figured she was probably picking up my clothes off the floor. She'd done this many times before. Just like Horse, she knew the routine and knew what her role was. When I got out, she had a towel laid across the sink. I dried off and walked into the bedroom, where she was sitting on the bed.

"I'm sorry okay? I just get scared, Dontay. I don't know what I'd do without you."

"What is it that you wanted to talk about?"

"Can you come here please, and sit next to me?"

I walked over to the bed and stood in front of her. "What is it?"

Her eyes were planted on the print of my dick showing through the towel that was wrapped around my waist.

"Stop it," I said.

"I'm sorry, but it's distracting," she said.

"Come on now, you made a whole scene so I'm trying to understand why."

"Can I tell you after?"

"After what?"

"After I suck it?" She bit her bottom lip.

Instantly my dick was hard. She always knew how to quickly change the subject. I couldn't turn down that offer, even if I was annoyed with her behavior. I grabbed the towel and let it drop to the floor. I took a few steps close to her meeting her lips. She wrapped her lips around it without touching it. She moaned as she sucked it like a Popsicle. I couldn't take it. I grabbed the back of her head and fucked her face. Every time my dick hit her tonsils I felt the cum brewing. I tried to hold it back. I'd taught her well. Who would've guessed that she was a virgin when I met her? It didn't take long before I was cumming and she was swallowing it. Not even a drop escaped. She continued to suck until the sensitivity was too much for me. I backed up.

"Stop it, damn," I said.

She began to laugh. I was still standing there trying to get myself together.

"Dontay, I'm pregnant," she blurted out.

"What did you say?" I asked. I wanted to make sure I was hearing her correctly.

"I said I'm pregnant."

Damn, I wasn't ready for that. Just like that, everything changed.

Chapter Twenty

Sexual Healing

Desire

Two weeks had passed since I told Dontay I was pregnant, and I hadn't seen or heard from him since. Since he split his time between Tracy and me, I figured that was where he'd been staying. I knew bringing up the subject would most likely turn him away so instead I decided to reel him in with sex or something close to it.

I walked into my bathroom and drew a tubful of hot water with lilac-scented candles lit to relax. I was horny and the hot water against my skin would give me the illusion of his warm body on top of me. I slid down into the water and grabbed my cordless phone off of the floor. I hesitated before dialing his number but I needed a fix and hearing his voice would have to suffice. It took a few rings before he answered, and I almost burst hearing his deep tone through the receiver.

"Hey, baby, are you busy?" I quizzed him as I rubbed my hand over my left leg.

"I'm just sitting here watching a movie. What's up?" he asked, obviously attempting to throw me a hint.

"I miss you. I haven't heard from you." I couldn't resist letting out that tad bit of information.

"Really?" he quizzed me. "So did you need me to do something for you?" he asked, trying to cut the conversation short. I wasn't about to get off of the phone that easily.

"Actually I do," I spoke lowering my voice to a seductive whisper. "I want to make love to your ear!"

"What's that?" he quizzed me, attempting to dodge my comment.

"I want you to listen while I imagine you here with me. Is that okay?"

"Who, Tracy? She's right here lying across my lap." He fumbled trying to inform me of her presence.

"I don't care if she's there. All you have to do is listen."

"Okay, go ahead and tell me what happened," he responded, giving me my cue to move forward.

I continued using that seductive tone that caught him in the first place. This tone was enough to make any man hard as a brick. I was aware of my talents long ago and had been able to snag many men in the past, even men who were attached.

"I wish you were here so I could feel you caressing me. You begin to remove your clothing to join me. I sit in the hot water watching as the steam rises from the tub. I'm getting excited as each part of your muscular body is revealed. Damn, I want you, and I lick my lips, anticipating tasting you. Once you are fully undressed, you fondle your manhood as I continue to pant, waiting for your hardness to meet my lips. You take your time moving closer to me, forcing me to wait a little longer. I part my lips widely enough to make way for you, and you slowly push your thickness inside of my wet mouth. My tongue massaging your shaft forces you to let out a sigh. I begin to massage my clit with one hand as I use the other one to play with your balls. You taste so good as I feel your hands on the back of my head, easing me into a deep throating routine. I stick two fingers inside of my tunnel as I crave you inside of me. Can you feel me, baby?" I quizzed him as I caressed myself imagining the scene that I was describing.

"Yeah, I feel you. What happened next?" he spoke quickly.

"You remove your manhood from my oral cavity, and it's missing your presence already. You stroke your length from end to end and pull me from the tub. I follow your lead, and you kiss me long and sensually, as I could feel your member pressed against my body. Damn, I want you inside of me, and I grab hold of it to let you know just how much. You bend me over, with my hands using the tub to brace myself, and you slide in from behind. Your girth has been missed, and I moan with satisfaction as you fill me up completely. The sound of you moving in and out of me intensifies the excitement. My tunnel quickly provides more lubrication as you increase your speed. I scream, 'I love this dick!' over and over again the way you like it, and you tell me exactly how much you love this pussy as you push down on my back to create a deeper arch. Are you feeling me, baby?" I asked as I continued to move my fingers in and out of my wetness.

"Oh, yeah! So then what?" he asked excitedly.

"You remove your length once more long enough to pick me up and sit me on the edge of the sink. With much force you dig deep inside of me with my legs open wide allowing you the space to fit all ten inches inside. I wrap my arms your neck and look into your eyes. I rise up to get close enough to lick your lips. I savor the taste as I beg for you to go faster. You oblige, and I am satisfied with the tempo. I yell, 'Fuck this pussy!' over and over again as you continue to keep up the pace. I don't want you to stop, and I pray that you can hold on a little while longer. I can feel myself nearing an orgasm as you go to a slow stroke with circles hitting my G-spot. I moan for you to keep it right there as you continue the movement. I can feel you throbbing inside of me letting me know that you are close to your peak. I want us to cum together so I wrap my legs around you giving you a direct hit of my spot. 'I feel it, baby. I'm cumming, I'm cumming,' I yell as you explode inside of me. We stand there holding on to each other as I know that I am completely satisfied. Are you satisfied, baby?" I quizzed him as I removed my cum-covered fingers from my burrow.

"Most definitely," he spoke honestly.

"Who is that, baby? I thought that we were going to watch the movie together," Tracy spoke in the background.

"We are," he responded.

"Now," I said, "when you get time, please come over so we can talk. There's more where that came from."

"Cool. Thanks for letting me know what happened. I appreciated that."

"I love you," I said before hanging up the phone.

A few hours later he came through the door. I knew that it would work. I was sitting on the side of the bed putting on lotion when I heard him coming up the stairs. Before he could even say anything I stopped him.

"Listen, I understand that you aren't ready for a child, trust me I do. I'm not really ready either, but I don't want to have an abortion. If you decide that this is the end for us then fine, I'll deal with that."

"I'm not saying this is the end for us, but I have to sort some shit out. There's a lot going on right now, and not just with Tracy either. It's just bad timing, and I think it's unfair to bring a child into the world like this. I just came here to get a few things, then I'm leaving."

"Leaving? After all of that? You really came here to throw salt in the wound. Why would you come here and do this to me?"

"There are some things about me that you don't know. I know for a fact if you did, you wouldn't want to deal with me. I just haven't told you because I didn't want to hurt you, but maybe it's time that I did."

"What the hell is that supposed to mean?"

"The man who killed your brother, that was the man I worked for okay? All this time I knew that, and I never said anything. The man who shot you, all of it, I knew."

I sat there silent trying to make sure that I'd heard him correctly.

"I'm sorry, all right? I gotta go."

He turned his back and walked out. I was frozen. I didn't know what to say or what to think. Granted, I had been seeing other people because he did, so I should've been happy that he was leaving. Those things I could get over, but what he'd just said was ripping me in two. I couldn't even cry after it all set in. I wasn't sad. I was angry. What was I supposed to do now?

Chapter Twenty-one

Ready

Alisha

After the incident with Jay, I was still on edge. I had nightmares for two weeks following the tragic confrontation. Hope was just as traumatized. Neither of us had ever faced the barrel of a gun, and seeing someone's head explode is a vision I was sure neither of us would ever forget. Despite the effects, we pressed forward with our wedding plans. As I stood in front of the mirror, looking at the couture Allure Bridals gown as it hugged my curves, I was flabbergasted. This gown was well worth the $8,000 price tag.

"Hurry up, girl, before I get too drunk off this champagne!" Hope yelled from the showroom.

"Seriously, Alisha, you know how I get when I drink too much," Tasha yelled.

Tasha was one of my bridesmaids and Desi's younger sister. Since the start of our relationship, Tasha and I had always gotten along. There were times when people assumed that she was my blood versus his. She'd even stepped up for me a few times when Desi and I were at odds. I'd grown to love her just as much as I loved him. I truly believed that she'd always be there for me even if my relationship with Desi failed. I took a deep breath before I stepped out on the platform. Both of their mouths dropped once they saw me.

"Oh, my God, Alisha, that dress is fucking sick. You look drop-dead gorgeous," Hope said, immediately setting her glass down on the table and walking over to me.

"My brother is going to lose his mind when he sees you in that shit."

"Umm, thanks for the compliments, but could y'all stop with the profanity? Y'all are killing her ears," I said, pointing to the sales associate who was clearly offended by the language.

"I'm sorry, but this is me, shit," Tasha said, shaking her head.

"I apologize for their rudeness," I said, looking over at the pale woman whose cheeks were beet red.

"It's totally fine," she responded.

I knew she was lying, but she surely didn't want any trouble. I continued to twirl around and look at myself in the mirror. Hope and Tasha continued to tell me what they both thought Desi was going to do to me on our wedding night. Of course they didn't sensor themselves and kept it 100 percent explicit. After I changed back into my clothing and paid the remaining balance, we headed out of the store.

"So where are you two headed now?" Tasha asked.

"Probably back home. I still have so much to do," I replied honestly.

"Aww come on, let's go to the bar or something. You won't be single for long. Might as well enjoy it before Desi locks those cuffs on your ass." Tasha laughed.

"I'm down. I don't have shit to do," Hope blurted.

I shot her an evil eye. She knew I hated bars. After going through the shit we went through with Jay, I was trying to stay out of places that could potentially bring drama my way.

"Aww come on, Alisha, stop being an old maid. Let's have a few drinks then I'll let you go, I promise," Tasha said, pulling on my sleeve.

She made a puppy dog face and a whimpering noise trying to convince me to go.

"Okay, just a few," I finally agreed.

I really did have a ton to do, and I liked to be waiting for Desi when he came home. A cold bed will make a nigga search for a warm one. I reached in my bag to grab my cell phone. I wanted to send Desi a quick text message to let him know that I was going out. I always tried my best to let him know my every move. I never wanted him to wonder. I was honest with him because I had no desire to be with any other man but him.

We got into our cars and headed down to a local lounge called Déjà Vu. This was Tasha's favorite spot. I wasn't a huge fan of local spots, because they often were filled with the same people I tried to keep my distance from. When we pulled up, there were a few people hanging around outside, but from the amount of cars parked in the lot I knew that it had to be packed inside. I felt totally underdressed as I walked in and found wall-to-wall men in expensive gear and women scantily clad. Bitches always went the extra mile to get attention. I shook my head as we made our way through the crowd, and over to the bar.

"Give me a double shot of Patrón," I said to the petite barmaid. I needed to get tipsy quick if I was going to enjoy myself in this environment.

"Really? That's how you feel?" Hope laughed, sitting down on the stool next to me.

"Girl, yes, if I'm going to tolerate this ratchetness in here."

Tasha laughed. "Girl, maybe I can grab me up a boo thang. There's always some prime meat up in here. A bitch can stand some good dick tonight."

I looked around the bar after I threw back my shot. The burning going down my throat caused me to shake a little. Both Hope and Tasha laughed at me. I wasn't a big drinker, but I wasn't the nicest person when I was sober.

"Ooh, girl, don't look right now, but Dontay's fine ass just walked up in here with his entourage," Tasha said, taking a sip of her Long Island Iced Tea.

I slowly turned, and looked over to the crowd that followed him. No doubt he was fine and hella paid. I'd heard a lot about him, but had never actually met him. From what I'd heard, he was one of the most feared drug traffickers in the city, and he wasn't one to fuck with. I knew scamming him could mess around and get me killed, so I never sought him out.

His diamonds glistened all the way across the room. I found myself staring, almost mesmerized by his presence. I bashfully turned away when we locked eyes. I was practically a married woman, yet salivating over this man. He had this aura that was hard to ignore.

"Girl, I'd suck him from sun up to sun down! You hear me?" Tasha blurted.

"You are a fool," I replied, shaking my head.

"Aww, this is my shit," Hope said, getting up from the stool while quickly drinking the rest of her drink and slamming her cup down on the bar.

She pulled me off of my stool toward the dance floor. Tasha followed me. Once we were on the floor we began dancing to the beat. I was feeling good. Floating off the Patrón was definitely lowering my inhibitions. I was doing my best twerking routine as Hope and Tasha encouraged me to continue. I had the full attention of everyone in the small lounge, and I loved it. The center of attention was where I loved to be.

Before I knew it, they were doing the last call for alcohol. I didn't need any more to drink, but I went to the bar to sit down and rest my feet while Tasha and Hope went to the ladies' room. I was looking down at my phone when I was startled by a deep voice in my ear.

"Can I get you a drink?" a tall, dark-skinned brother said over the loud music.

"No, I'm good, thank you."

"Aww, come on. You can let me buy you a drink."

"No, really I'm fine. I have to get up early in the morning."

"Just one," he said, touching my hand.

"The lady said no, thank you." Dontay was now standing in between us.

The annoying bugaboo retreated without another word. Dontay turned to face me. "You cool?" he asked.

"Yes, I'm fine. Thank you." I smiled. I tried not to stare at the chain dipped in black-and-white diamonds. I was sure the price of it was well over fifty grand.

"I'm Dontay," he said, sticking his hand out to shake mine.

"I'm—"

"Alisha. I know who you are." He laughed.

I was taken aback. How the hell did he know me? I knew my name rang bells, but I certainly didn't think they chimed loud enough for him to hear. I stuck my hand out to meet his.

"How did you know my name?" I asked.

"Because I know everything. I have my ear to the streets. Nothing gets by me," he said, still holding on to my hand. "That's a nice rock you got there," he said, looking at my engagement ring.

"Thanks," I said politely, pulling my hand away.

"You getting married?" he asked.

"I thought you knew everything," I replied sarcastically.

"I was just fucking with you to see if you'd be honest. I know Desi really well. He's a lucky man."

Again, I was speechless. I wasn't quite comfortable with him knowing so much about me. Granted, I knew a lot about him, but I wasn't all up in his personal business.

"What are you? Some sort of stalker?" I asked with a twisted lip.

He burst into laughter and held his chest as he continued to crack up at me for almost a full minute. "Stalker? I ain't never stalked no woman. I'm the man in these streets! If you don't know, sweetie, you betta ask somebody." He continued to laugh.

"I'm just saying you know an awful lot about me, that's all."

"Don't flatter yourself. I know an awful lot about everybody."

I sucked my teeth and turned around in my chair. I was tired of the conversation and hoped that Hope and Tasha would show up any minute.

"Well, Alisha, you enjoy your night, a'ight? I gotta run," he said before walking away.

I didn't even say good-bye. Don't flatter myself? Really? He knew I was the shit. Why else would he have come over in the first place? A few seconds later, Tasha walked over to me with one hand on her hip.

"What were you doing talking to my future baby daddy?"

"Girl, please. Nobody wants him. Some asshole was over here annoying me, and I guess he overheard the convo. He asked him to step off. That was it."

"Oh," she replied. She didn't seem 100 percent satisfied with my answer, but it was the truth. Though Dontay was fine, I wasn't interested in his arrogant ass.

"Let's get out here. I'm beat," Hope said.

We left the lounge and headed over to the parking lot. I spotted Dontay sitting on the hood of a black Mercedes with a cigarette in his hand. He looked over at me and chuckled. I kept walking over to my car, got in, and drove out of the parking lot without giving him a second look.

Chapter Twenty-two

Salt in the Game

Alisha

"Two more days until I become Mrs. O'Neal," I said, smiling while rubbing my hand across Desi's chest.

"Are you ready?" he asked.

"Ready as I'll ever be. I can't wait until you see me in that dress." I sat up in bed.

"Yeah, Tasha told me how good you looked in it. I'm excited. Never thought I'd be getting married for real." He laughed.

"Well, I'm the type of bitch you get and keep," I replied.

"You know you killing my pockets. You've spent almost a hundred grand on this wedding."

"I know, baby, but I'm only getting married once. I want the wedding that I've always dreamed of."

"That's for damn sure. You're always gonna belong to me," he said, leaning in to kiss me. "I gotta roll. Got some shit to take care of. I'll check on you throughout the day," he said before getting up and heading to the bathroom to take a shower.

After he was dressed, he kissed me and left. I smiled as I watched him walk out of the bedroom. I was ecstatic about becoming his wife. My fairy tale was finally coming true. I looked over at my cell phone that had a few missed calls from Hope. I'd been so wrapped up in my morning lovemaking that I hadn't made my wakeup call. I dialed her as I got up to look through my closet for something to wear.

"Hey, girl. Sorry I missed calling you this morning."

"Did you listen to my messages?" she asked with worry in her voice.

"No, I just called you instead. What's up?"

"Well, I heard through the grapevine that Dontay's been asking a lot of questions about you. I think you need to do some damage control before he fucks up your wedding."

"Huh? Why the hell is this fool so worried about me? He doesn't even know me! Prior to that night at the lounge I never even had a conversation with him!" I yelled into the phone.

"I know, but I also know what kind of nigga he is. When he sets his sights on something, he doesn't stop until he gets it."

"But I don't know what he wants. Do you know where I can find him?"

"Not really, but maybe we can slide through the lounge. I heard he's always in there."

"Let's do that tonight so I can see what his problem is."

"All right, I'll come over around nine. Cool?"

"Yeah, that's cool."

I was furious. I thought about asking Tasha if she wanted to go, but after the way she reacted the first time I decided that might not be a good idea. Especially when I was set to marry her brother in just two days. I was focused on things going perfectly. I had some running around to do during the day and Tasha was meeting me at the florist in less than an hour. I hurried and made it there just in time. She was patiently sitting inside of her car waiting for me.

"Hey, boo," she said as she got out and walked over to hug me.

"Thanks for coming. I just want to make sure these flowers are perfect. I really appreciate your help, seriously."

"It's no problem at all."

We went in and chatted while we waited for the florist to finish with a customer.

"Guess what! I finally got Dontay's number, and we're supposed to link up this weekend." She smiled.

Under any other circumstances I'd be happy for her, but until I figured out what his ulterior motives were I just couldn't be. "Oh, yeah? That's what's up. I really hope it works out for you. I know how much you like him."

"Girl, I'm obsessed with that man, and he doesn't even know it. I mean, I've had a crush on him since I was a teenager." She laughed.

"Obsessed? Girl, you might not want to say that out loud again." I laughed. I wanted to tell her what Hope had told me, but she'd probably take it the wrong way and assume that I was jealous. I was happy with my man. Although Dontay was a great catch, I wasn't interested.

"I'm just joking. I'm not really obsessed. I'm just glad that I'm finally going to get a little quality time with him."

"I hope it turns out to be worth the wait." I smiled.

The florist was finishing up with the customer and went into the back of the store to retrieve the flowers that I'd had Lisa order. The flowers exceeded my expectations. They were perfect in every way. Things were shaping up nicely, and this wedding was going to be the talk of the town for years to come.

After leaving, Tasha and I had a quick lunch before parting ways. I made a few more runs before going home to get dressed for the lounge. As promised, Hope arrived at nine, and we were on our way.

The parking lot was packed as usual. I looked around to see if I could spot the Mercedes that I'd seen Dontay sitting on the last time, but it wasn't there.

"I hope he comes, because I really need to talk to him."

"He'll be here, I'm sure," Hope said, adjusting her dress as we made our way over to the entrance.

Once we were inside, I did a quick surveillance of the room. I couldn't spot him or any of the men he usually brought along with him.

"Do you see him anywhere?" I asked Hope as we both took a seat at the bar.

"Nope, not yet."

I tried to remain calm, but inside I was losing it. I just wanted to settle whatever this thing was so I could continue with my plans. After a few drinks and songs later, I noticed him entering the building. I tapped Hope on the shoulder, interrupting her conversation with the guy seated next to her.

"He's here," I said.

"Go talk to him."

"I am. Be back in a minute," I said as I slid off the stool.

I took a deep breath as I walked across the room. It was tight so I had to excuse myself at least fifteen times before I made it over to the VIP section. There was a guard standing at the front to keep all the patrons on the outside of the red rope. Dontay stood up when he saw me and walked out of the VIP section to greet me.

"So, to what do I owe this pleasure?" he asked, rubbing his right hand across his beard.

"I came to talk to you because I heard that you've been asking a lot of questions about me. I'm getting married in two days, and I really don't need any drama on my wedding day."

"You're right. I have been asking about you, but it's really harmless. I'm not trying to fuck up your wedding, especially if you really plan to marry him."

"Yes, I really plan to marry him. I don't get you or what you want from me."

"I just want to get to know you," he said, stepping closer to me.

I immediately backed up a bit. The last thing I needed was someone running back to Desi and telling him that this nigga was all up in my face.

"Listen, I'm practically a married woman. I don't need to get to know any other niggas, okay?"

"I know you think you have it all, but I know for a fact your man ain't got it like me. I also know he ain't slinging his dick like me either," he said, moving in on me yet again.

Once again I backed away. "You have got to be the most arrogant man I've ever met in my life. My man treats me very well, and he knows how to satisfy me."

"Listen, I just want to get to know you better and let you get to know me. I guarantee one night with me will change your mind. Matter of fact, you can even get married, but you'll still be feening for me." He was so close I could smell his breath, which smelled like Winterfresh gum.

"Thanks, but no thanks, okay? I'd really appreciate it if you'd stop questioning people about me. Have a nice evening, Dontay," I said before walking away. He grabbed my arm and stopped me. "Let my arm go," I yelled.

He laughed as he released his grip and put both of his hands in the air. I rolled my eyes and turned to walk away. I walked smack into Tasha who was standing in my view with both arms crossed and an evil stare.

"I can't believe you!" she yelled.

"Can't believe what?" I asked. I wasn't sure how long she'd been standing there, but there really wasn't anything going on—at least not on my part.

"After I told you how I felt, you had to get in the way."

"Tasha, what are you talking about?" I asked, confused. I hadn't gotten in the way of anything as far as I knew.

"He called me this afternoon and cancelled. Said he couldn't see me," she continued to yell. Her face was frowned so tight you could see every wrinkle. I was honestly embarrassed because people were beginning to stare, including Dontay.

"What does that have to do with me?"

"He couldn't see me because of you. Because he wants you!" she yelled.

"What?" I asked. I was shocked and appalled.

"You are marrying my brother in two days. Two days, Alisha, yet nothing has changed! You're still the same scheming bitch you were before."

"Really, Tasha? Whoever is giving you information is totally misinforming you. I don't want Dontay. I have a man I love deeply. The fact that you could stand here, disrespect me, and accuse me of shit I'm not guilty of lets me know you were never really my friend to begin with."

"You're nothing but a liar and a backstabber. Clearly you were never really my friend either," she yelled as she turned around and stormed off.

She'd lost her fucking mind. I was beyond embarrassed as everyone continued to stare at me. Hope came over with a look of total confusion.

"What was wrong with Tasha? She just stormed out of here like a bat out of hell."

"She accused me of messing around with Dontay. First, I'm not interested in him and, second, how the fuck is she mad at me over a nigga who doesn't even belong to her? She can kiss this friendship good-bye. She's lucky I'm dressed in Gucci or I would've slapped her ass. I'm so fucking pissed right now. Let's just go."

I began to walk toward the exit. I couldn't wait to tell Desi about his sister's behavior. He was sure to take my side and set that bitch straight. I hadn't done anything wrong. I deserved respect, and I was going to get it one way or the other.

Chapter Twenty-three

Friend or Foe

Alisha

"What do you mean he's not coming?" I asked, hysterically crying. I could barely breathe, and my chest was growing tighter with each passing second.

"His sister called and said he wasn't coming and you'd know why," Lisa, my wedding planner, said with a look of pity on her face.

I was dressed and ready. There were 200 guests sitting in their seats waiting for me to walk down the aisle. There was no way this could be happening to me. This had to be a nightmare! I desperately needed someone to pinch me and wake me up. Was Tasha really that conniving? Or, even worse, was Desi that gullible to believe the bullshit that she said?

"Call him again," I screamed. My makeup was a mess. I kicked off my shoes and began pacing the floor.

"Still no answer," Hope said, holding her cell phone in her hand.

"Try again." I continued to scream and pace the floor. Here I was in this beautiful gown with mascara running down both of my cheeks.

"You have to calm down, Alisha," Hope said.

"Calm down? How the fuck do you expect me to calm down when my fiancé has yet to show up?"

"I understand, Alisha, but they can hear you. I know you don't want your guests to know what's going on."

She was right. I didn't want people to know what I was going through. I was devastated. Hope continued to call his phone to no avail. She also called Tasha who wasn't answering her phone either.

"This can't be happening," I said as I sat back down. My anxiety was over the top. I felt like I was near passing out. I sobbed uncontrollably. I was never the emotional type, but I couldn't hold it together.

"Alisha, what would you like me to tell the guests?" Lisa asked, standing near the door with her notepad in her hand.

I didn't respond. I felt lightheaded, and soon felt my body sliding out of the chair and down to the floor. When I woke up, I was still in my wedding gown in the back of an ambulance on my way to the hospital. I tried to remove the oxygen mask from my face only to be told to leave it on. I looked over to my left at Hope who was sitting with the paramedic.

After being taken into the emergency room, I was examined and released. I'd merely passed out because of my hyperventilating. Hope informed me that Lisa was taking care of the guests who were in attendance. Most of them were under the impression that the wedding was postponed because I was taken to the hospital. The truth was that Desi had left me and had not answered anyone's calls.

I was hit with another blow when I arrived home. All of his things were gone. He'd actually packed up and left. I dialed his phone over fifty times trying to get an explanation. I left messages until his voicemail was full. I'd called every one of his friends as well. All of them claimed to be oblivious to his location.

I called Tasha because I really wanted to give her a piece of my mind. I'd never wanted to physically harm someone so bad in my entire life. She'd completely ruined my fucking life. I'd never seen someone so desperate for a man. I wanted to kill that bitch!

I couldn't understand how he could just pack up and leave without even speaking to me or giving me a chance to explain myself. For the next three days, I stayed in my bed. I didn't even take a shower so you know a bitch was depressed. Under the circumstances, I didn't give a rat's ass about washing up. All I could think about was how my life had spiraled completely out of control.

I thought back to everything I'd experienced growing up. I was never given a fair shot. My mother was the meanest and most heartless woman alive, and not having a father set us up for failure. After my brutal attack and subsequent abortion, I was angry at the world. I wanted every man to suffer for the shit the Johnson boys did to me. I spent years taking niggas for everything I could until I met Desi and decided to change for the better. None of it mattered. Regardless of how much I changed, there was always someone or something waiting in the wings to pull my ass back in.

Weeks passed, and I still hadn't heard from Desi. To make matters even worse, I was given a notice to vacate the property. I had ten days to find a place to live. I didn't have much money set up, and I didn't have anyone to call besides Hope. Luckily, she had some connections and a few thousand dollars to get me an apartment. Once I was all moved in, I promised her that I would pay her every penny of what I owed her.

At that point, there was no turning back. I'd be dammed if I was going to continue to beg Desi to talk me. He'd made his choice so now I'd make mine. I scrolled through my phone and made a list of all the ballers I needed to contact. Fuck niggas; get money. The bitch was back.

Chapter Twenty-four

Stack of Dough

Alisha

Looking down at my watch, I knew I was running late for my meeting. If there was one thing that I hated, it was being late, but the previous night's events had me so exhausted. I didn't roll out of bed until after three p.m. I was dressed to kill in a slinky black dress and a simple pair of black platform shoes. You could never go wrong with all black.

My jewelry was simple, silver with rhinestones, and my hair was laid so I was both irresistible and fabulous. I was on my way to see O, or Omar. Omar was one of the top hustlers in the city. I mean this nigga had as many minions as the dude in the movie *Despicable Me*. Although there was something extremely sexy about a man with power, this was strictly business.

I had been seeing Omar ever since my breakup with Desi. Omar had been the nigga to get me back on my feet, because shit got tight when Desi moved out and forced me out on the damn street. I bounced back fast with his help, and I'd been bouncing on his dick ever since.

I headed straight to the bar when I arrived at the restaurant. I ordered two shots of Patrón and another shot splashed with some pineapple juice. I needed to get tipsy fast. Otherwise, the night might not go the way I'd planned.

Omar had a wife whom he'd been with for over ten years. From the outside looking in you'd think they were the perfect couple. They had the perfect house, the best cars, and four beautiful kids. His wife, Ashley, was beautiful no doubt, but what she lacked was the ability to fuck her man like he needed to be fucked. That's where I came in. I was damn good at what I did. I'd learned how to maneuver my body in ways that most women weren't capable of. Therefore, he was like putty in my hands.

I waited patiently and bobbed my head to the sounds of the live jazz band. They were jamming, and I was feeling good from my drinks. Every now and then I'd be approached by a man and offered a drink, but each time I declined. I needed to be ready to do what I came to do.

After another twenty minutes had passed I was becoming annoyed. He was already almost forty minutes late. I was just about ready to walk out when I spotted him and his wife being escorted over to their table. I wasn't sure if he'd noticed me so I grabbed my phone out of my clutch to send him a text message.

Once he sat down I noticed him going into his pocket to look at his phone. His wife looked over at him, and appeared to be questioning him about the sender of the message. I was anxious. All I could think about was fucking his fine ass. I had to remain calm, at least until he could break away from his woman. I kept a strong stare until he finally noticed me, and our eyes met. He nodded to the left, giving me the signal to meet him out back.

This had been our meeting place for the past three months and, ironically, it was their set date night for the past three months as well. Believe it or not, I wasn't a threat to her, because I didn't have any intention of being his girl, or anyone's, for that matter. After losing Desi, my only priority was to get paid. Surprisingly, that had been working out for me perfectly.

I stood up from the barstool and quickly swallowed the remainder of my drink. I watched Omar walk toward the rear of the restaurant. He was friends with the owner so it wasn't out of the norm for him to walk through the restricted areas that customers weren't typically allowed in. I walked right past the table where his wife was seated, and we both looked at each other, and gave a smile.

If this bitch only knew I was about to walk out of there and fuck her husband, she'd wipe that fake ass smile off of her face.

Once I reached the dark parking lot in the back of the restaurant, Omar was sitting on the hood of his car waiting patiently for me. It was about to go down, and my stomach was full of butterflies, just as it always was when doing something so risky.

Without speaking, I walked over to him and stood firmly in between his thighs. I seductively licked my lips, and then stuck my tongue out so he could bring his lips closer to mine. He did as I expected. As he moved in closer, he opened his mouth and quickly took my tongue inside of it. His thick tongue was warm, causing me to get extremely moist down below. His hands caressed my ass as he raised my skirt. His dick was rising and trying to force its way through his jeans. That was my cue to unzip his jeans and release it.

I rubbed the tip of it. As I playfully backed away from him, I stuck my fingers into my mouth and sucked the pre-cum off of them. He smiled while his dick dangled freely. He reached into his pocket, pulled out a condom, and quickly put it on.

Cars were driving by the street at the end of the dead-end block, but once he bent me over the hood and stuck his dick inside of me, they were no longer a part of my world. I bit my lip as he moved in and out of me with force.

I liked it rough, and the intensity of possibly being caught made the shit feel even better. I continued bouncing my ass back against him as he firmly gripped his hands around my waist. You could hear the echo of his body bumping up against mine. The faster he went, the louder the sounds grew. After a half hour of friction, I was nearing an orgasm and the pulsing of his stick let me know that he was too. He increased his speed and dug deeper inside of me before pausing to release all of his juices.

As his body shook his grip got tighter. He let out a few moans as he tried to hold it together. Each time we met the sex was better than the previous encounter. I looked forward to my end-of-the-week treat like a child waking up on Christmas knowing there were gifts waiting under the tree. He was my Santa, and always bought good dick and cash as presents.

He slowly pulled his dick from inside of me before speaking. "You are on birth control, right?" he asked while removing the condom and tossing it over into the lot.

"Yeah, why?" I asked as I stood up to fix my clothing.

"'Cause the condom broke and I didn't realize it," he responded while zipping his pants back up.

"Oh, yeah, it's cool, we're safe." I smiled.

"Well, come give me a kiss before we go back inside," he instructed.

I moved closer to him and met his lips for a kiss. I was excited when he slipped a wad of money into my purse before going back into the restaurant. Once we were inside, we parted ways. I headed over to the ladies' room to get myself presentable before leaving.

I wet a few paper towels to clean myself off. Then I retrieved my makeup and comb from my purse to fix my hair, and touch up my face. As I was reapplying my red lipstick, I thought back to his comment about the condom breaking. I'd brushed it off so he wouldn't get bent out of shape, but it wasn't cool by a long shot.

"Shit!" I said aloud.

I hated when that shit happened. What good were the fucking condoms if they broke more often than not?

After my quick temper tantrum, I got myself together. There was no need to cry over spilled milk. I would pick up a morning-after pill just to be on the safe side.

After being satisfied that my look was in order, I left the restroom. I walked back past their table before leaving as if I didn't even know him. Shit, she could have him as far as I was concerned. I got what I needed: dick and a stack of dough!

Chapter Twenty-five

The Title

Alisha

The following morning I woke up to the annoying sound of the alarm clock. I damn near knocked the clock on the floor trying to turn it off. I had a nine o'clock appointment at the hair salon, and I needed to be on time or else I'd be in there all damn day. Going to the hairdresser once a week was like a job. I'd never worked a regular nine to five so my patience was short when it came to being in one place for too many hours. I had been sick the previous week and missed my appointment.

Mina was my stylist and since she was one of the hottest in the city, her book was always packed. She'd been styling my hair since I was a teenager, and I didn't trust anyone but her to touch my mane. I threw on a pair of faux leather shorts and a crop top since it was going up to ninety degrees outside. I always had to be fly, just in the event I ran into a baller. When I wore shorts and stilettos, I had niggas under my spell immediately.

I strutted in the salon in perfect time. The shampoo girl was waiting for me. After my hair was blow dried, I hopped right into Mina's chair.

"How are things going?" Mina asked while brushing through my hair.

"Everything is great. I'm living it up as usual! You know how I get down," I replied with a giggle.

"I'm glad to see you doing better after being in the hospital."

"Yeah, I'm good. I'm glad to be out of there. That flu really kicked my ass! That two-day stay was two of the hardest days of my life, besides the day I was left at the damn alter. I'm just glad that's all over with, and it's back to business."

"Girl, you are the same Alisha, always about them dollars!"

"That ain't never going to change! Shit, this is me! Anyone who doesn't like it can kiss my ass!" I replied as we both began laughing.

She began to style my hair as I sat there looking out of the window at this chocolate brotha making his way toward the shop. His jewels were shining, and that shit was ringing like a cash register in my ear. I wished that I were up walking around so he could see my ass jiggle, but my hair was still only halfway done.

He stopped at the receptionist's desk, and she pointed in my direction after he bent over to ask her a question. Every bitch in the building had her eyes on him. He walked directly over to me. I was speechless, wondering how he'd pinpointed me. I was the shit, but there were about fifteen other chicks in here and my hair wasn't done. Not to mention the cape that was covering my sexy-ass curves.

"Hey, how are you doing? Are you Alisha?" he asked, flashing his pearly whites.

"Why? Who wants to know?" I asked with sass. I couldn't have him thinking I was like these other thirsty, drooling bitches.

"He said you would be sassy," he said.

"Excuse me?" I sat up in my chair.

Mina immediately stopped brushing my hair.

"My boss, Dontay, wants to meet with you. He told me to stop by here and give you this," he said, passing me a small bag from Tiffany's. "The address and the meeting time are on the card." Without another word, he walked away.

I sat there stunned. How the fuck did Dontay know where I'd be, and what the hell did he want to meet about now? He'd been a huge part in the demise of my relationship with Desi, though I blamed Tasha for making something out of nothing. But being the businesswoman I was, I figured that meeting up with him could be beneficial for me. Especially since I was no longer with Desi. All eyes were on me in the shop with the anticipation of seeing what was in the bag. Mina's nosy ass even abandoned my hair and was also waiting for the reveal.

I pulled the box from the bag, which contained a charm bracelet and necklace set. *This nigga doesn't even know me that well, and he is already spending that change. He's definitely my type of man!*

I pulled out the card that read: *Meet me at seven sharp, at the warehouse on Cambria.*

After reading the note, I was about ready to jump out of the chair. I wished that Mina could hurry up and finish my hair so I could go change, because I was definitely going to be there at seven, and I was damn sure going to be sharp!

Getting niggas to spoil me was something that I had become a professional at. I ran into a few roadblocks along the way, but I always managed to find my way around them. Since I'd witnessed my mother being trashed by men, I vowed to avoid following in her footsteps.

Instead, I was going to flip the script and take these niggas for everything they had. As far as my taste in

men, first came the money and then the looks. I needed a
fine-ass thug, but I needed them to be paid first! Without
the dough, the looks weren't important. Everything I
wanted I could get, and it came to me easily. All I had to
do was flex my ass in front of a nigga and he'd be crawling
to get a piece. Once they were caught up, I would take
the money and run. I went years before I fell in love with
Desi, since love wasn't something I strived to achieve.

After finishing my runs for the day, I rushed home to
change. I was out of the house in record time and not a
hair was out of place. I drove down to the warehouse that
was on the card. I figured it was the spot where his workers packaged and shipped his inventory of cocaine. I was
nervous as I approached the guards who were standing
post outside. I had on my freakum dress of course, since I
wanted to leave a good impression. The guards searched
me, and opened the door to let me in.

As soon I walked in, I noticed Dontay standing toward
the back. I switched over to where he was with a strut
that had everyone's attention. Niggas were practically
drooling over the ass as I walked past. He turned to look
me up and down a few times before speaking.

"Well, well, well, if it isn't the infamous Alisha. You
look damn good! I can see why the niggas are losing their
dough to you. That nigga Desi created a monster," he
said, smiling.

I nodded, returning the smile while holding in the urge
to curse his ass out. Talking about Desi was off-limits. It
wasn't a topic that I liked to revisit.

"I know you're wondering why I asked you to come
here."

"Yeah, I'm definitely wondering about that," I
responded.

"Well, first, let me thank you for coming. Did you like
the gift?"

"You are welcome and yes, I loved it, but I'd rather skip the small talk and find out exactly what it is you want from me."

"I see that you are all about business, and I like that. That shit is a turn-on, if you know what I mean! I tried to come at you before on a personal tip, but this here is something different. You're sexy as hell when you're mad. You know that?" he said while laughing, before noticing my evil stare. "I'm just fucking with you, ma. Let's go to my office so we can talk. You don't have to be all serious and shit all the time," he said, beginning to walk into the direction of his office.

I wasn't always this serious, but I wanted him to believe that so he wouldn't think that I was a pushover and attempt to take advantage of me. We entered the plush office that looked like it in no way belonged in the back of a warehouse. It looked more like something you'd see on HGTV or some shit. The office had thick beige carpet and a large cherry-wood desk with a coffee-colored leather chair. He had a huge gun cabinet with at least ten guns in it, and a large plasma TV on the wall. The pictures from *Scarface* and *The Godfather* displayed his strength. Shit like that turned me on, because I knew a nigga who worshiped them was bound to display some of their characteristics. I walked around the room for a few minutes before sitting down in the chair opposite the desk. We stared at each other for a few seconds before he spoke. I was anxious to hear what he had to say.

"So, I've heard about the way you like taking niggas' money! I think that shit is foul—"

I cut him off, because starting off the conversation dogging me was definitely not going to keep my attention. "Listen, if that's all you called me here for, I can turn around and walk out of here."

He straightened up in his chair. "Well, what do you think I brought you here for?" he quizzed me.

I was irritated, and I damn sure wasn't in the mood to play the guessing game. I began to rise up out of the chair without saying a word.

"Where are you going?"

"Look, my time is very valuable. I could be out somewhere getting paid!" I spoke loudly. "I wish you would just cut the bullshit and tell me why I'm really here!"

"Have a seat and I'll explain," he said, pointing in the direction of the chair I previously sat in. "I know your game, and I need someone like you on my team. I'm trying to make this a win-win situation for both of us."

"What could I possibly do to help you and your team?"

"All I need you to do is be yourself. I'll designate the niggas, and you just need to work your magic. It's pretty simple."

"I still don't understand how that will help you."

"I've been in this game for a long time, and I'm pretty successful now, but I have to eliminate my competition in order to move to the next level. Complete takeover."

"Eliminate?"

"Yeah. I have to get rid of them permanently if you know what I mean. Here's a list for you to look over," he said, sliding me a small piece of paper.

"No, I don't know what you mean. All I do is get with these niggas and make them spoil me. Simple as that. The shit you are talking isn't something I want to get involved in. I'm not going to jail for murder!" I stood from my chair.

"You won't go to jail, I promise that."

"I can't, I'm sorry. I just can't be a part of this. I'm sure you'll find someone else willing to do it."

"I don't want anyone else to do it. You are the best one for the job."

"I'm sorry. I just can't," I said before walking to the door.

I couldn't believe what he was asking me to do. I had plenty of other ways to get what I wanted, and killing someone was just too extreme. My mind raced as I got into my car.

What the fuck was I thinking going there in the first place? I knew about Dontay's boss status, and I also knew how much he was feared. He was paid and that's what attracted me, but the devilish grin he displayed as he slid me the list of names turned me off. One name in particular rang in my ear, and I wasn't going for it.

I was still very much in love with Desi, and there was no way in hell I'd set him up to be killed. I walked out of that office and left the conversation right where it was, in his twisted-ass mind. Once I made it home I decided to call up a few of my money trains to get a couple of dollars. I became a little bit annoyed when none of them answered. My day wasn't going the way I'd planned since I thought by then I'd be lying next to a warm body with a fat pocket. After an hour of trying, I gave up and took my ass to bed. There was always tomorrow.

Chapter Twenty-six

Late Nights, Early Mornings

Alisha

The following day, I woke up and immediately checked my cell phone for missed calls. There was only one number on the list, and I didn't recognize it. I dialed the number to find out which one of my gravy trains had called to apologize. If there was one thing that I hated, it was being ignored. Even though most of them were hustlers and often were truly busy, I should always be a top priority. Shit, the top-quality head and pussy I gave them should have had them dissing their mommas to talk to me.

In addition to the amazing sexual techniques, I also knew some of their dirtiest secrets. If pushed, I could ruin their lives. I sat up in bed as I waited for someone to answer the phone. A deep voice finally boomed through the receiver. I loved a deep-voiced man. That plus a pocket full of cash was a sure way to get me out of my panties.

"Hello, did someone call Alisha from this number?" I asked in a seductive tone. I was hoping that this was my next money train.

"Yeah, this Dontay. Did you think about my proposition?"

Instantly my stomach began to feel nauseous. A feeling of anxiety came over my body as I contemplated hanging up. There was something about his voice that made it difficult to end the call though. It was almost as if I were mesmerized, but afraid at the same damn time.

Dontay wasn't a person you'd want to cross. He was highly feared in the streets, and I certainly didn't want another gun in my face. Especially since Desi was no longer around to rescue me. I decided it would be best to listen to what he had to say. I sat in silence waiting for him to speak again.

"What's wrong? Cat got your tongue?" he asked.

"No, I'm just wondering what the hell you're calling me for since I told you I didn't want anything to do with that shit," I said, hoping that he'd just forget about it and look for another bitch to do his dirty work.

"That was yesterday, and shit changes. I just wanted to make sure you were serious about declining my offer, because I won't ask you again. Besides, I know you're running low on cash since most of the niggas you typically use as a bank won't return your calls."

"Well, you're misinformed. I haven't even called anyone and my men call me back," I lied.

"I told you before, I know everything. I call the shots out here in these streets. All I had to do was inform them of your scandalous-ass past and pad their pockets with a few dollars and, poof, they agreed to drop your ass. Now you need me."

I sat there for a second in shock. Had he really contacted them? Did he really have that much pull? I silently asked myself a million questions while he giggled in the background. I wasn't ready to accept defeat, but I wasn't trying to go to jail for the rest of my life for fucking with him. I was too young, too wise, and too damn fine to be Big Brenda's bitch. He was a damn fool if he thought that my only means of making money was being his slave. I was determined to prove him wrong.

"Fuck you, Dontay," I spat.

"Oooh, I love it when women talk like that. That shit makes my dick hard! But listen, if you think you don't need me, and you truly believe you can make it on your own out here I wish you the best of luck. When you realize that what I'm saying ain't bullshit and your ass is broke and busted, holla at me."

Click.

I sat there looking at the phone to be sure that he'd actually hung up on me. I began to scroll through my call log to see who'd answer. Again, all of my calls were ignored and some sent me straight to voicemail. I wasn't sure what to do. I started to think that maybe I could just do the job and get my life back. Possibly get close to him and turn the tables. Hell, he could be my next victim. I wasn't giving up that easy. I was born to fight.

I got up and sprung into action. If I was going to do this job for Dontay, it would be on my terms. I looked through my closet for some of the sexiest gear that I could find. I settled on a pair of high-waist black pants with a see-through cropped top. I threw on tons of accessories and pulled my hair back into a ponytail. I finished off my look with a pair of black platform pumps and a pair of vintage shades. I looked good enough to eat, and I could see my ass up on platter with Dontay's faced buried in between my legs apologizing for treating me as he had.

I headed straight for the warehouse where we'd previously met. I was focused. I had something to prove, and I wasn't going to be satisfied until I'd gotten what I came for. I parked and walked over to the door where, as before, the guards were standing post. I removed my shades so they could see my face.

"I'm here to see Dontay," I said with confidence.

"Dontay ain't here," the taller one replied.

"Well, there's his car so I know he's here, and I need to see him. Tell him Alisha's here."

"I know who you are, but like I said, he ain't here. So turn your pretty little ass around and get back in your car before I pick you up and put you in there myself," he said as he stepped closer to me.

I could feel his breath on my forehead. I was extremely uncomfortable, but I wasn't going to let him know that. The other guard was laughing and looking down at his cell phone.

"You know, I don't see what's so funny," I blurted out looking around the guard who was practically on me he was so damn close.

The second guard looked up at me and immediately frowned. "Who the fuck do you think you're talking to, bitch? Keep that shit up and I'll rearrange that face of yours."

I sucked my teeth and dismissed him with my hand. He laughed again and looked back down at his phone. The taller one began to speak again. "Listen, go ahead and get in your car and roll. I'd hate to see some bad shit happen to you. A chick like you doesn't belong around here. This is a man's world. Around here, bitches get hurt or end up dead trying to stomp with the big dogs. I'll tell Dontay you were here."

I briefly looked him over and pondered my next move. I decided that I was going to leave, but I'd make sure to come back every day until either he let me in or Dontay came to find me. Without another word, I walked back to my car. I decided to go back to my apartment to change and come up with another strategy for reaching Dontay.

I walked toward my building and headed down the hall. I sensed that someone was following me because each step I made they did the same. I began to pick up the pace to reach my door near the end of the hall. As soon as I got to the door, a hand covered my mouth, which was followed by a whisper in my ear.

"You were looking for me, now I'm here. Open the door," Dontay demanded.

At first startled, I was immediately annoyed when I heard his voice. I snatched away from him and turned around to look him in the eye.

"Why didn't you just talk to me at the warehouse?" I questioned.

"Because you came unannounced. You needed to know that you don't just pop up on a nigga."

"Like you're popping up here, right? At my damn house, unannounced?"

"Listen, you came looking for me. What is it that you want?" he said, moving closer to me.

His lips were practically touching mine. For fear that I'd accidentally kiss him, I didn't move.

"Why me, Dontay?"

"I already answered that question. You're the best one for the job, but I won't beg you."

"Why are you here?"

"I answered that question already, but I decided I'd give you one more chance to change your mind. The fact that you came looking for me lets me know that you're considering it."

"I don't trust you. I feel like you're setting me up to take the fall for you."

"You don't trust me? Really?" He gripped my waist with both of his hands, immediately sending chills up and down my spine. "How about now?" he whispered.

I didn't respond. I didn't trust him and probably never would, but that wouldn't erase the fact that he was sexy as all hell. He was irresistible and he knew it. His confidence was through the roof, teetering on arrogance.

We were in a stare down, neither of us blinking. He licked his lips once while keeping his hands in place. I couldn't take it any longer. His body heat was warming my insides and causing extreme wetness in between my legs. I threw caution out of the window and grabbed the sides of his face, kissing him intensely.

We were going at it like two ferocious beasts. You could hear the echo of our moans trickling down the corridor. His hands were caressing my breasts through my blouse and the stinging of my erect nipples told me that they were harder than they'd ever been before. I couldn't wait any longer. I pushed him off of me, and we both stood silent for the five seconds it took me to open the door and walk inside. The door slammed causing me to jump. I turned around to find him stripping off his clothing at the door. I followed suit and almost grew scared when I saw the size of his dick, which was now bouncing freely in the air.

Fuck it. I was a big girl, and I was going to handle his dick like it was size of a pinky. He walked over to me and immediately backed me into the nearest wall. The force of our bodies hitting the wall knocked a few things off of the end table including a glass candy dish that shattered immediately.

With his strong, chiseled arms he picked me up off of the floor then positioned me on top of his dick. My wetness slid down his shaft and the tightness of my tunnel caused him to moan. I wrapped my arms around his neck as I bounced up and down on his dick.

"You like this dick?" he asked.

I was silent, trying to enjoy the pain, which hurt so good.

"I said, do you like this dick?" he asked, thrusting inside of me with tremendous force. I thought for sure he'd entered my cervix.

"Yes!" I screamed.

"Then tell me you like it. I need to hear it!" he said, continuing his assault on my vaginal walls.

He was punishing this pussy like it was a student who'd been bad in school. He was digging deep like a gravedigger digging a grave. He wasn't even holding me up with his hands, but instead balancing me on his muscular thighs. Each time my ass slapped against them, it echoed throughout the quiet apartment. I knew what he wanted. I'd heard his request, yet I remained silent. I was stubborn. It was my nature.

"I'm gonna stop unless I know you like it. Matter of fact, if you don't love it you can forget bussin' a nut," he said as he continued to ram his dick into me.

"I like it," I said, finally giving in. There was no denying the fact that the dick was unbelievable. He was hitting spots that I didn't even know existed.

"I said I need you to love it," he yelled, picking up speed.

"I love it," I whispered.

"I can't hear you."

"I said I love it." I raised my voice an octave.

He stopped midstroke allowing me to rest with all ten inches inside of me. "I'm done then," he said.

"No," I whined. No way was he really going to stop.

"I told you what I needed."

"I love it, dammit! Now fuck me!" I screamed.

He immediately resumed his attack on my inner walls. I moaned with pleasure. I could feel my body tensing as it neared an orgasm. I wasn't ready just yet, but I couldn't control it. My eyes were squinted tightly, and I bit my bottom lip bracing myself for the eruption that was about to take place as swiftly he pulled his dick out of me, bent down, and rested my thighs on his shoulders before standing up and raising me damn near to the ceiling.

He grabbed a hold of both thighs with his hands and ferociously attacked my clit with his lips and tongue. My body released all of my satisfaction on his tongue and goatee. I was shaking uncontrollably and screaming his name. I tried to stop him, but he held on tight. I was almost brought to tears as my body trembled over six feet in the air.

After a few more minutes of torture he released his grip and pulled me back down. He licked his lips and smiled. He pulled me over to the sofa and bent me over before entering me from behind. With the same force he'd used previously, he moved in and out of me holding on to both of my arms from behind using them to pull me in closer. I was hollering like a newborn baby, but out of pure pleasure. I was in wonderland, never experiencing dick so damn good. He moved in all directions never slipping out of me once. I came at least four more times before he removed his throbbing dick and released his warm cum all over my backside. I was frozen. My body had never experienced a session as exhausting as it was invigorating.

"Where's the bathroom?" he asked.

I stood up and pointed toward the hall that led to the bathroom. "Second door on the left. Washcloths are in the cabinet behind the door."

He returned a few minutes later to put on his clothes as I went in the bathroom and cleaned myself up, quickly returning with a robe on. He was fully dressed and looking down at his cell phone when I returned.

"So what does this mean?" I asked. I wanted to know if our sexual contact meant I no longer needed to do the job he was asking me to do.

"What are you asking me?"

"I'm asking if I'm off the hook."

"Listen, the sex was great and I'd definitely love to hit it again; however, I'm a businessman, and I still have a business to run. I still need your help."

I was speechless. I didn't know why I ever thought he actually had a heart. Clearly he was the most heartless bastard I'd ever met in my life. I felt sick to my stomach. I felt tears building up, but I wouldn't allow them to make it to the surface of my tear ducts. He was leaving me no choice. I had no other means to make money and, just as he said previously, I did need him, because I had no one else.

"Don't stand there looking all sad and shit. This is a great opportunity for you. You're gonna have enough money to take care of yourself, and if you do what I need, you can be on my team for life, you feel me?"

"What do you mean for life?"

"I mean, I'll have your back and this thing we have, we can turn it into something else."

Hearing that made me feel a little bit better about the situation. I understood that business came first. I knew this from my relationship with Desi and the countless other romps I'd had with hustlers. I needed a strong man in my life.

Losing Desi was devastating to say the least. Scheming and scamming kept a few dollars in my pocket, but it wouldn't get me the house on the hill. Only the title of wifey could get me that. Maybe this was my ticket back to the top. Back to the lavish life that I so desperately needed to return to.

"So what are you gonna do?" he asked.

"Whatever you need me to," I responded.

"Good," he said before walking over to me. He grabbed me by the chin and kissed me on the lips. "Come to the warehouse tomorrow at two, and I'll tell you what I need you to do."

"Okay," I agreed.

He left without another word.

Chapter Twenty-seven

Traumatized

Alisha

Two Weeks Later

"Thanks for bringing me here. This is a really nice restaurant," I said as I sat down in the chair and slid up to the small table covered in white linens.

"No problem, shorty. I don't mind spending my money on someone as fine as you," Joe said as he smiled.

I stared at him from across the table. I must admit I was pretty turned on. Joe was one of the sexiest thugs I'd seen in a long time. His caramel-colored skin was smooth as a baby's ass. His hair was shaped up to perfection, and his body was tight.

I could tell that he worked out often by how ripped he was. I knew that this was only a job but I also knew I had to at least screw him once before Dontay's plan of elimination went into effect. The longer we sat and talked, I felt sorry for Joe. Underneath all of the gangsta shit, he seemed like a good man.

Joe was a major figure down West Philly. He pushed cocaine throughout the area gaining him a lot of respect and plenty of cash. He practically had the neighborhood known as The Bottom sewn up. He was well known throughout the city, so I'd heard his name once or twice before, but I had never had the opportunity of meeting him until now.

Dinner didn't last very long since we were both anxious to get to the hotel. I didn't really eat much since food hadn't been agreeing with my stomach lately. I was wearing a dress that hugged my size-eight frame. Joe was all over me as soon as we hit the DoubleTree hotel. His hands were all over my back as we stood at the counter waiting for the room key. I was growing more excited as we walked to the elevator.

Once inside, he backed me against the wall and pushed his body against mine. His hard dick was pressed up against me as he placed his lips onto mine, right before pushing his tongue through. When the elevator opened, he quickly grabbed me by the hand to guide me to the room. My heart was beating fast, and my panties were getting wetter by the second.

After entering the room, he walked me over to the bed and bent me over, immediately pulling my panties down. He dropped his pants and massaged his dick to keep it at attention until he was able to open the condom and put it on. I was patiently waiting with my ass still up in the air. He slapped his dick across my ass a few times before shoving it inside of me. He filled my insides completely, and I moaned extremely loudly while he continued to move in and out of my juicy tunnel.

"This pussy is so fucking good!" he whispered in excitement.

I contracted my walls to hug his dick while he hit my G-spot continuously. He slapped my ass over and over again while holding on to my waist like a handlebar with his other hand. He used his strength to go deeper and deeper as I begged for more. He was wearing me out and appeared to be unfazed by the workout.

Once I reached my climax, I was ready to stop since the constant pounding was going to have me walking like a cripple for days. I tried to slow him down a bit by making slow circles, but that didn't work.

Damn, this nigga was fucking me like a racehorse. He pounded with extreme force and speed for over a half hour in the same position nonstop. I wondered if his ass drank a Red Bull or something, because he wasn't slowing down a bit, not even for a second to catch his breath.

He was still banging my back out when I heard a loud boom. Afraid, I ran to the nearest closet and tried to hide when three huge men in black ski masks kicked the door in with their guns drawn. Two of them grabbed Joe, while he was fumbling with his pants to retrieve his gun, and began kicking him. I sat in the corner crying hysterically when the third guy came over and picked me up off the floor.

"This is a fine bitch here. If he didn't already fuck her, I would have sampled this pussy!" he said before he began laughing.

The other two joined in the laughter as he pushed me down on the bed and began tugging at my shirt to get a peek at my breasts. I didn't know what to expect as I lay there trembling. I wanted to fight, but I was positive I would be killed. I was so scared that even my teeth were chattering. I kept an eye on the door waiting for one of them to turn the other way allowing me to get up and run out of there, but that time never came. There was no way I could get past them. I instantly had flashbacks of the Johnson boys.

While Joe was being beaten, I prayed that I would make it out alive as I closed my eyes and quickly said a silent prayer.

"Shut the fuck up!" the tallest one yelled at Joe, as he continuously told them they could have whatever they wanted.

"You see your punk-ass man over there? He can't even protect you!" he yelled, gripping the back of my hair and pointing in Joe's direction. "Answer me, bitch!" he yelled.

I sat there silent still in shock, while he screamed obscenities. I was afraid to speak and risk saying the wrong thing since I didn't want to piss them off even more than he clearly already was.

"Get up, muthafucker, and face me like a man!" the shortest one yelled at Joe.

As Joe stood up and turned around to look at me, a few tears fell from my eyes. Blood ran down his face and his right eye was damn near swollen shut. I felt sorry for him as I continued to cry. I noticed a strange look on his face, and I couldn't tell what it meant. Either way, I knew that it wasn't a look of submission, and I was afraid of what would happen next.

Joe balled up his fist and knocked the shorter one off his feet. As he tried to attack the one left standing, the taller one let go of me and quickly ran over to interrupt their tussle. He put the gun to the back of Joe's head and immediately fired. The silencer that was attached muffled the sound of the shots. I screamed and jumped up off the bed to try to escape. I was quickly pulled back into the room once I got one foot out of the door.

"Where the fuck are you going?"

"Please let me go. I promise I won't say anything," I cried.

"Sit your ass down. Ain't nobody going to hurt you! Take this phone and wait for the call," he said, passing me a prepaid TracFone. "If you call the cops before that call comes through, we'll catch your ass and kill you. Do I make myself clear?" he yelled.

"Yes," I said, speaking for the first time since they'd entered the room. I just wanted this to be over and would say anything to get them to leave.

"Take care! And stop fucking with punk-ass niggas like him!" the shortest one said before they made their way to the door.

I watched them like a hawk without moving. I ran over to Joe as soon as the door closed to see if he was still breathing. I leaned over him and told him how sorry I was when I realized he was dead. I would have never wished this on my worst enemy.

I was glad to still be alive, but I was traumatized yet again by murder. I contemplated calling the cops, but I knew that they meant business by what'd just happened, so I opted to wait for the phone call. I sat there on the bed hoping that someone would have heard what was going on, but no one did. I waited ten minutes and when the call came, I didn't know what to expect.

"Hello," I said nervously as my voice trembled.

"Good job, baby!" Dontay yelled through the phone.

"What, Dontay? You set this shit up?" I yelled in anger.

"You should have known that. I told you what the plan was so I don't know where the confusion came in at!"

"You could have at least warned me!" I screamed into the receiver. "I thought that my life was over!"

"I'm sorry you were scared, but if I would have warned you, you would have probably fucked everything up by acting suspicious. I'm proud of you."

"Fuck you!" I screamed.

"Maybe later, but right now I need you to call the cops and tell them what happened. They'll come talk to you, and you tell them what went down. Once you get home, holla at me, and I'll let you know what's next."

"I'm not doing shit for you after this! I mean it!"

"Look, you're upset and that's cool. We had a deal, and I know that money sounds good to you right about now since you're damn near broke! Just do what I said and everything will be cool!"

Click.

"Dontay! Dontay!" I yelled into the phone before realizing that he hung up.

I was furious that he risked my life the way that he had. He never told me that I would be caught in the crossfire. I never expected to witness any murder nor did I expect to be degraded in the process.

I called the cops as I was ordered. It was the hardest thing that I'd ever done. To sit and lie about a man's murder and possibly risk going to jail for my part in all of it was difficult. Just thinking about what'd just gone down made me sick.

I couldn't even sleep that night. I tossed and turned for the week that followed. It took awhile for me to get back to Dontay, but I had to do what I had to do. Dontay made sure of that.

Chapter Twenty-eight

Secrets and Lies

Alisha

I had been feeling sick for days following the incident with Joe. Although I had been keeping up with my meds, they weren't working very well. I was weak, nauseous, and had a fever a couple of days in a row. I continued to take Tylenol to bring my temperature down, which only worked temporarily. I couldn't possibly work for Dontay feeling as lousy as I did so I went to the clinic for a walk-in visit to see if I could get a different prescription.

The clinic was packed as usual, and I kept my shades on to avoid being noticed by someone I knew. I signed my name on the board and sat down. I was getting annoyed the longer I sat. I looked up at the clock and before I put my head back down to glance at the magazine I'd been flipping through, I noticed a girl named Shena from around the way. I wondered what the hell she was doing here. I definitely didn't want her to see me, but I soon realized that it was too late.

"Alisha, is that you?" she quizzed me, before walking over to where I was sitting.

"Hey, Shena, how are you?" I said before removing my sunglasses.

"What are you doing here?" she asked, though she probably already speculated.

"Girl, I had to come pick up something from the doc."

"Why are you on this side? You know what section this is, don't you?"

"I know, girl. There weren't any seats on the other side," I lied.

"Well, there are some seats now. You don't want people to think you got something!" she said, pointing out a couple of seats on the opposite side of the waiting area.

"You go ahead, girl, I'm cool right here."

"All right, well, I'll be seeing you around," she said before walking away.

Shena and I had never been friends in any way so for her to think we would get all buddy-buddy so she could find out my business was out of the question. Her name was called shortly after that, and I was glad since I didn't want her to see me be called back. I sat in the room for about ten minutes before the doctor came in.

"Hello, Ms. Washington. What brings you in today?" he asked before sitting down on the stool in front of me.

"The medicine that you gave me before I left the hospital isn't working. I'm still having the same symptoms. I haven't even been able to hold any food down."

"I can adjust the dosage and maybe that will help, but you already know that your condition has advanced, and there isn't much that we can do at this stage. I can prescribe you some other things that may keep the nausea under control along with it. Are the fevers still coming as well?"

"Yes, I just take the Tylenol to bring them down."

"Has that been working?"

"Yes, temporarily. I'm just tired of being sick."

"Well, as I've said, I'll change the dosage on the meds, and hopefully that will keep you comfortable."

"Okay," I replied.

He wrote out my prescriptions, and I went straight to the drug store to have them filled. I decided to rest for the remainder of the day to get myself together. I knew that I would probably be feeling much better the following day and able to get back on track.

But soon it was back to business. Dontay had me setting up at least one nigga a week. Eventually, I became immune to the fear. When they would come kicking the door down, the feelings I displayed weren't much more than an act. Dontay was paying me well for my time, but I was looking forward to the big payoff at the end and the faster I got it, the better off I'd be.

Chapter Twenty-nine

Working Girl

Alisha

I was a month away from completing the last job and Timmy was next in line. Timmy wasn't the "take you out to dinner and a movie" type. Timmy liked to be alone to just relax. He wanted to show me the place where he went to clear his mind, and since I knew it would be secluded I was game.

"So why didn't you get at me a long time ago? I mean, I'm a fly-ass nigga, and you chose all of those wack niggas before me." Timmy spoke while glancing at my figure, which was showing through my tight-fitting attire.

"I didn't really think you'd dig my style. I thought I might have been too flashy for you," I replied before sitting down on the park bench beside him.

"Too flashy, never! Who could be flashier than me?" he said, laughing as he flipped his collar up on his shirt. I joined in the laughter, as I knew that he was absolutely right.

He was a flashy nigga. He had diamond chains, watches, earrings, and pinky rings. He wanted it to be known that he was paid. I'd never really paid Timmy any attention since I ran into him around the time I was with Desi. Had I met him first, I would have definitely given him a sample of the kitty cat.

Timmy was from North Philly and had the area practically sewn up. Niggas all around knew about him, so before Dontay no one would even think about stepping into his territory. Timmy's weakness was women. A nigga like Timmy would give up the dough without hesitation, and that's what I needed in my life. He wouldn't be caught dead with a chick who wasn't as fly as him.

"So what is it that you want from me?" he quizzed me, with a smile on his face.

"I'm trying to be with you," I lied, trying to gas him up.

"With me? You mean like my girl or something?"

"Yeah. Why, is that a problem?"

"I mean, we've been kicking it for a couple of weeks now, and I dig you. I just don't know if I'm ready to be with you."

"Well, I'm definitely not one to beg, but I dig you too. That's why I hollered at you in the first place."

"Is that right?" he said before placing his hand on my thigh. I knew where this was headed, and I was all game for it.

"Baby, let's head to the car, so I can show you something," I said in a low, seductive tone.

Timmy jumped off the bench before I could even finish my sentence. We walked back to the car, which was parked a few feet from the park bench. After we got in, I went to work immediately, loosening his belt to get to his bulging manhood. Once I pulled it out, I was shocked and excited by the size.

I massaged its length while he laid his chair back and put his hands behind his head. His dick was at attention waiting for me to kiss it. I licked the tip of it before wrapping my lips around the head, sucking on it. He moaned a little as I took the pre-cum into my mouth. I was soon deep throating his stick while playing with his balls at the same time. My pussy was so wet, and I couldn't wait to feel him inside of me. I picked up the pace, and he loved every second of it. I wanted him to fuck me as I pulled my panties to side. I stuck two fingers into my juicy tunnel. I finger fucked myself waiting for the orgasm that was nearing. I continued to suck his dick while moving my fingers in and out of my pussy until I exploded. The juices began to pour out and when I was finally able to open my eyes to speak.

Bang! Bang!

The glass from the window shattered all over my head. Blood sprayed everywhere. I jumped up to move close to the passenger side when I was forcefully pulled through the window of the car. Blood was all over my face and hands as I stood up straight.

"Get the fuck in the car!" the familiar voice yelled at me.

I didn't waste time running over to the black Expedition parked on the side with the ignition still running. Though I expected them to come, I could never fully prepare myself to witness a murder.

The two men grabbed Timmy's lifeless body from the car while the third man opened up the trunk. The two men threw him into the trunk of his car and slammed the hood shut. The last man pulled out a can of gasoline and poured it all over the car. Next they lit a couple of homemade bombs, quickly throwing them inside of the car and causing it to burst into flames. As the three of them jumped in, I sat quietly in the car. I didn't know where the hell they were taking me, and at that point I didn't care. I needed to be done with this shit, and I was one more job away.

We pulled up to a huge house off City Line Avenue. I figured that it must've belonged to Dontay since I noticed his Benz parked outside. Once they pulled up, they beeped the horn then instructed me to get out. I obeyed, but stood there still for a few seconds before Dontay came to the door.

"Come on in," he motioned with his hands.

I had my arms folded across my chest with sadness in my eyes. I didn't want to do this anymore, because it was breaking me down. He tried to wrap his arm around my shoulder, and I quickly pulled away.

"You don't look too good, baby. Are you okay?" he asked.

"No, I'm not okay. What kind of a fucking question is that? They just blew a man away while I had his dick in my mouth! Do you think I would be okay after some shit like that?" I yelled. "Where is the bathroom, Dontay? I need to clean myself up!"

He stood there staring at me for a few seconds. "You sure you don't want to talk?" he asked, trying to show his sensitive side.

"All I need is a shower, a towel, and a washcloth!" I replied loudly.

"No problem. I'll show you to the bathroom," he said as he began to make his way toward the stairs.

I was shaken, as the thoughts of Timmy slumped over replayed in my mind. Once we reached the bathroom, he reached into the linen closet to hand me a towel and washcloth. I waited for him to walk out so that I could close the door behind him. I sat down on the toilet seat to remove my shoes and clothing.

After turning on the shower I waited a few seconds for it to reach the right temperature. As soon as the hot water hit my skin, I began to cry. I cried because I was sorry that I'd ever gotten involved with this. I had witnessed too many murders. Though I was no longer afraid of the situations, inside it was breaking me down. I had to build up the skin to handle the situations, and I had done pretty well with it. I was just growing annoyed with the fact that he'd been stringing me on for the past few months, telling me it's just one more job. Each time he would tell me the same thing.

I had begun to care about Dontay, and it was hard for me to walk away. The first time we had sex I knew that I needed to be around him. He never acted as if he cared about me, but I knew better. It was all a cover-up. Instead of pushing him away, I fell back, hoping that when this shit was all over with, something good would come out of it.

Dontay had a way of reeling me back in even when I was furious with him. At one point in time, it was me putting people under a spell. Now I was stuck in that position. I was going to get my game back one way or another. Dontay wouldn't be able to stop me.

I heard a knock on the door, and I noticed Dontay's naked body through the glass door of the shower. It was just like Dontay to try to fuck after a situation like that. I didn't say a word as he stepped into the shower behind me. I knew that I could use some dick, so I wasn't going to turn him away no matter how angry I was.

He rubbed his hands across my back, and I began to shiver imagining the scene that was about to play out. His hands felt good and the feelings that I tried to avoid were bursting through. I could feel his lips on my back as I pushed my face completely under the shower. He wrapped his hands around my waist and pressed his hardness against my ass as he held me tight.

"Do you want me to fuck you?" Dontay whispered into my ear.

I could barely speak, but was able to moan, "Yes," as his fingers traveled down to my clit. As much as I hated him for getting me involved in this life, I embraced his strength.

Dontay always took control. It was that persona that won me over in the first place. He wrapped his hands around my neck, not tight enough to hurt me, but just enough to get my adrenaline rushing. He sucked on the side of my neck before questioning me once more.

"You really want me to fuck you?"

"Yes," I said as I reached around behind me to grab hold of his dick.

I stroked the length of it as he continued to play with my clit. I put one leg up on the side of the tub to give him full access. He took advantage of it by sliding his finger inside of my wetness. I sighed as the warmness of his fingers sent chills through my body. He continued kissing the back of my neck as I ground my hips to get his fingers deeper inside of me.

"I need you inside of me now," I moaned.

He turned me around and looked me eye to eye. We didn't speak, but as our lips met, we both knew what the other thought.

The water was beating on my back as he continued to push his tongue into my mouth. At that point, I didn't care about the anger that I'd felt earlier. All I cared about was feeling his dick inside of me. Without hesitation, he turned me back around, bent me over, and shoved his stick inside of me. The feeling was intense, and he picked up speed once he realized how much I was enjoying it.

"You like this dick?" He panted as he placed his hand on my back digging deeper inside of me. I couldn't speak as I was nearing an orgasm.

"I said, do you like this dick?" he repeated, obviously annoyed by my silence.

"Yes, dammit! Just don't stop!" I responded loudly.

He was hitting all of the right places. Dontay was the best dick I'd ever had. I knew that it wouldn't be long before he came since I was throwing my ass back at him, contracting my walls at the same time. I had learned a long time ago that there weren't too many men who could take what I called a recipe to put a nigga to sleep.

He removed his length from inside of me then released on my ass. I was satisfied, but I didn't know where it would lead. I knew that Dontay wasn't one for serious relationships. Neither was I. I just hoped that maybe all that I'd done for him would somehow steer him away from having me being an accessory to any more murders.

Dontay quickly washed himself off, and without saying a word he stepped out of the shower. I followed his lead then met him in his living room.

"So, does this mean that I won't have to do any more jobs for you?" I asked nervously. I was breaking down, and he'd just witnessed the effect this life was having on me. I hadn't told a soul about what I was doing for him. Not even Hope knew. I couldn't risk going to jail so I kept my lips sealed.

"What gave you that idea?" he said before taking a puff of his cigarette.

"I thought that you saw what this was doing to me. I thought that you hopping in that shower with me was showing me that you cared."

"Look, I wanted to tap that ass 'cause I love fucking you. You were ass naked in my shower and since opportunity presented itself, I took advantage. It didn't have shit to do with caring," he coldly responded.

"What?"

"Look, I have a business to run. You are definitely an integral part of that. I don't mix feelings in with business. That's why I'm still standing and that's also why these niggas I'm setting up are going down. I love pussy, don't get me wrong, just not enough to let it interfere with my plans."

"So what if I said I was through?"

"That's not an option. You're only option is to do what you agreed to do."

"Dontay, I can't do this anymore," I yelled.

"Look, I know that you are upset right now, but if you want that twenty Gs, you'd better get yourself together."

"It's not about the money anymore. This shit is fucking with me mentally."

"I'll give you a week to get yourself together, that's the best I can do. After that, it'll be back to business."

I couldn't even respond. All of my anger was coming back, because I could see how cold he really was. I had to figure out a way to be done with this shit. I knew that ignoring him would only piss him off. I didn't even know who his next target was, but I knew that I didn't want to be involved.

I left his house and made my way home with all different emotions flowing through me. All I could do was wait around for his call. It was exactly a week later when he got with me.

Chapter Thirty

The Unthinkable

Alisha

After I made it to the meeting, I walked in without saying much. I gave him the look of death as I sat across from him in his living room. I knew that Dontay would try to pull a fast one on me, so I was ready for whatever he threw my way. With both of us having the same personality traits, we were destined to bump heads on most situations.

When he walked into the room, I had my game face on, and so did he. I was determined not to give in, but at the same time, what choice did I have? I was ready to say damn the contract, but was my life really worth it? I was ready to say fuck it all.

"So, are you ready for the next job?" he asked with a stern look on his face.

"No, I'm not ready, but I just want to get this shit over with," I replied.

"Your next target is the nigga Desi from South Philly."

"No, Dontay, you know how I feel about him. I thought we agreed that he was off-limits."

"I never agreed to shit. I just saved him for last! That nigga has to go, and there ain't no ifs, ands, or buts about it!"

"We didn't agree to that or I would have never gone through with this shit! I told you how I feel about him!"

"Look, I know what I agreed to, and you need to get on the ball so you can figure out how to get back in good with his ass! I want this job done, and I want it done right. I've tried to be cool, but Mr. Nice Guy is gone. If you don't do what you agreed to do, it's curtains!" he yelled.

"I'm through with this shit, Dontay! I told you from the beginning he was off-limits," I yelled in frustration.

"What the fuck do you mean you're through? This shit ain't over until you do what you agreed to do!" he responded.

"I never agreed to hurt him. I care about him, Dontay," I explained as I moved closer, still trying to convince him to end this charade.

"Let me give you a newsflash. He doesn't give a fuck about you. He dumped your ass before, and he'll do it again," he yelled, pointing his finger into my face.

"Dontay, please, let me go. I've done enough already," I begged as tears fell from my eyes.

"Don't start that shit, Alisha. We had an arrangement. That's the bottom line. You need to go home, get yourself together, and holla at me later. I'm not changing my mind so you can cut the tears short!" he demanded before heading toward the door to let me out.

"Dontay!" I yelled as he opened the door. "Please don't make me do this," I pleaded, grabbing him by the hand.

"I said all I have to say," he said, snatching his hand away and pushing me closer toward the door.

I continued to beg before walking out. I thought that I could wear him down and eventually get him to change his mind. As he pushed me out of the door, I knew that I was fighting a war that I would never win. I walked to my car crying hysterically because of the fact that I had no choice other than to finish what I had started.

I pulled my cell phone out of my bag and stared at it contemplating calling Desi and tipping him off. I scrolled through the phonebook and pressed call. The phone rang a few times before he answered. When I heard his voice, I instantly froze. So, instead of speaking, I ended the call.

"What the fuck are you doing?" I asked myself aloud before turning off the phone completely. I knew Desi would try to reach me and see why I had called.

Chapter Thirty-one

The Whole Truth and Nothing But

Desire

A woman named Alisha contacted me. I didn't know who she was or what she wanted with me. She told me that she had some information regarding Dontay that I would want to hear. At the very least, I was going to hear her out. By this point, I was through with him, and I wanted nothing more than to see him pay. The times that I'd spent with Dontay had been traumatic to say the least. When you are young and vulnerable, you never realize the things that you think you need are so far from that. I should've known a man like Dontay was no good for me, or anyone for that matter, but I was blinded by lust that I thought was love.

The meeting was set for five, and I arrived just short of it. We were meeting up at the local Starbucks near Temple University. I wasn't sure why she picked the location, but public was always good. I walked in with my sunglasses on and looked around. I wasn't sure what she looked like so I took a seat since I didn't see any black women anywhere in there. After five minutes, a woman in a black dress approached my table.

"Hi, are you Desire?" she said.

"Yes, I am."

"I'm Alisha, nice to meet you," she said before sitting down.

"So what can I do for you?" I had my guard up. For all I knew, she could've been working for Dontay. I didn't trust a soul.

"I have some information that could put Dontay away for a very long time."

I sat up in my seat. I liked the direction of the conversation already. "Continue," I said.

"I have a list of murders, along with photos, text messages, dates, times and all. I can prove that he was behind multiple murders. I can also prove that he is running one of the largest drug rings in the city."

"So how do you have all of this information?"

"Because I helped him."

"Helped him do what?" I asked. I was confused. Was she telling me that she was also a murderer? If that was the case, then what was there to stop her from killing me?

"Set people up to be murdered."

"Why would you do that?"

"In order for you to understand, I'd have to tell you the whole story and this isn't the place to divulge those sorts of details. I know you are involved with a man who's in law enforcement and this is why I have to be careful with the information that I give you. I don't want to mess with your career or life for that matter," she said.

She was stone-faced, but her eyes had so much emotion in them. I could see that she was being honest, and I wanted to trust in my gut feelings.

"Well, the fact that you've called me here means that there is something to listen to. I'm extremely interested in hearing the details, so when or where do you think would be best to meet and discuss?"

"How about later on tonight, around nine p.m. maybe?"

"That time is fine. Where do you want to meet?"

"Meet me by the old steel mill in Frankford. You know where that is right?"

"Yeah, I know where that is."

"Okay, then I will see you there tonight—and please come alone. I don't want to involve anyone else in this," she said before standing up from the small table.

"Okay, I'll see you at nine," I replied, watching her leave. Immediately, I picked up my phone and called Lamar to tell him about what had transpired.

"Lamar, are you sitting down?"

"Yeah, I'm sitting down. What's up?"

"You will not believe this. I just met with a woman who claims that she has all of the information that we need to put Dontay away for good. If she truly has all of the information she claims, we could probably even get the death penalty!"

"How do you know that she is legit?"

"I don't know for sure, but I just have a good feeling about this. I'm meeting with her again this evening. She said she will hand over all of the details at that time."

"Okay, well, where are you meeting her? I'll go with you."

"No, Lamar, I have to go alone. She said that I had to come alone."

"You can't go meet her alone. You have no idea who this woman is. What if it's a setup? What if she is really working for Dontay and it's all a ploy to get you alone and kill you? You're not thinking smart at all."

"Look, Lamar, you have to trust me on this. I know that you are concerned, but I need this. We need this. I have to go, okay? I will call you later on tonight and update you," I said before quickly hanging up. I didn't want to give him time to try to convince me to let him accompany me. I had to go alone. I had to make sure this was handled and handled today.

Chapter Thirty-two

Murder in the First Degree

Dontay

I looked around to see who was there in the booth where Jimmy sat. In the surrounding booths there were groups of guys. Some were known to me, while others were unfamiliar faces. With my mind was racing, all I could think about was walking up to him, pointing the gun at his chest, and blowing him away.

I finally believed that this was the right time. I had been patient waiting on the perfect time to handle this important business. I had made a lot of bad decisions in my lifetime, but this wasn't one of them. For me this was right. It was his just due. I could've easily hired someone to do it for me, but then I'd never get to see the fear in his eyes once he realized that his life would soon be over.

The club was packed. Wall-to-wall people were every-where. I walked in and greeted a few people. I wasn't trying to conceal my identity. I didn't care who saw me. In fact I wanted to be seen so people would know that I wasn't the one to be fucked with. If that wasn't already known, this would surely be conformation of it.

As I made my way through the crowd to Jimmy's table, he looked at me as if he'd seen a ghost. Maybe he saw his reflection in me. Unfortunately, my good looks were a direct result of his good genes, because I looked just like him. That was something that made me hate him even more. Immediately he stood up once I reached his booth. There were no words exchanged at first, just grimacing looks. It was almost as if he knew what I had come to do. At this point, Lamar wasn't there, which was a good thing since he really didn't have anything to do with it. I couldn't hold him accountable for the sins of his father unless he tried to intervene. Then he'd be a casualty of war.

We stood there eyeing each other. I wasn't sure what was going through his mind, but for sure he was uneasy. I couldn't say that he was scared, but it definitely wasn't a comfortable situation.

"Well, well, well. I figured we'd meet again," he said with a fake-ass grin.

I wanted to slap it clean off of his face, but I kept my composure. "Again?"

"Yeah, I saw you driving by. I'm sure you know that nothing goes unnoticed."

"So you know who I am?"

"Of course I do. You're the spitting image of me. So do you want to sit down and talk?"

"I didn't come here to have a fucking conversation."

"Well, what is it that you came here for?"

I didn't respond. I was thinking hard, and I needed to decide his fate quickly. I didn't trust him or anyone who worked with him so I could've been taken out if I got caught slipping even for a moment.

"So what did you come to do, since you've made it clear that it isn't to talk?" he said.

I stood there remaining quiet, still contemplating whether this was the right thing to do. There wasn't anything I wanted more in life than to make him pay. Deep down I thought this very moment would feel better. I thought that it would give me the same adrenaline rush as all of the other murders had but surprisingly it did not. People were all around the club, and it was almost as if no one even noticed what was going on. If they had, they played it off extremely well. After a few more moments, I pulled the gun out of my pocket and pointed it at his chest. A few people scattered all over while some ducked under chairs and tables. I heard screams, but I tuned them out to remain focused on the matter at hand. He didn't even try to save his own life. He didn't apologize. He did nothing but stare at me.

I squeezed the gun and let off two shots, which went straight through his chest. He stumbled back before he fell onto the pool table. I casually stuck the gun back in my pocket and walked away. I followed those who were trying to get out of the club, trying to avoid being shot. Most of them didn't know that I was the actual shooter.

I walked over to my car, got in, and drove off, heading home. I wasn't worried about security cameras. I wasn't worried about any of that. I didn't even try to hide the gun. I wasn't throwing it away or anything. I didn't care at this point what the future held. My one mission in life had been completed.

Things in my life had taken a turn and not for the good. Yeah, I was still getting money but my personal life was filled with nothing but drama. The day that I learned that Tyrese was Desire's brother I was stuck. What was I supposed to tell her? Even though I wasn't the one responsible for his death I was extremely close to the man who was. When I saw the look on her face, I knew that she would never forgive me for keeping that information for such a long time. I should've sensed that the end was coming soon, but I wasn't at all worried. I was the type of nigga who was built to last. I was more than capable of weathering any storm that came my way.

Chapter Thirty-three

Payday

Desire

I pulled up to the old steel mill right before I was supposed to. I looked around in the parking lot, and there wasn't a soul in sight. It was a pretty dark night, not too windy, not too noisy. It was actually pretty calm. I looked at the clock, wondering when she would arrive. There was so much riding on this. I mean my whole life depended on it. The truth could actually turn my life upside down, but I didn't care. I just wanted him to pay. I wanted it to be over. I wanted him to get everything he deserved: the same fate that he given to so many people. The people whose lives he took away would get justice once and for all. This would be exactly what I needed to survive and exactly what I needed to get, finally letting Tyrese rest in peace.

So there I was, waiting on her to arrive and sure enough she pulled up a few minutes later. She got out of the car with a large manila envelope. I wasn't sure what was inside, but I hoped that it was the information that I needed to turn over to the police. I unlocked the doors before she got inside.

She sat down and didn't say a word.

"So is this everything?" I asked, breaking the brief silence.

"Yeah, this is it."

"So are you sure that you want to do this?"

"Yes, I'm sure."

I needed to see it. I need to see one way or another who the true Dontay was. She opened up the envelope and passed it to me. I was nervous as I began pulling out the contents of the envelope. There were pictures of men I knew for a fact had been murdered. I looked at her wondering what her involvement was.

"Who are these people to you?"

"These are the men I helped him kill. He used me to set these men up only so that he could move in and take over the territory. At first I didn't know that he meant murder. I thought that he just meant to put them out of business when in all actuality he meant to put them out of business permanently."

"So he asked you to set them up? How?" I asked. I still wasn't quite sure what she was saying to me.

"Basically, he had me meet these guys, sleep with them, and put them in compromising situations only so that his men could come in and catch them off guard and murder them. I did that for him numerous times. Even when I begged to stop, he threatened me. He just wouldn't let me live without finishing the job."

"So why are you telling me this knowing that you were an accessory to murder? You could be put away for life."

"He should be put away for life, and I'm willing to sacrifice my freedom for that to happen."

"So are you sure this is what you want to do? Because if it is, I'll take it down to the police station right now and set things in motion."

"I'm definitely sure. I've thought about it over and over again. I thought about anything else that I could do besides this, and there's nothing. There is nothing that I could do other than wait on street justice, which could come now or not at all. This way, I know for a fact he's going down."

"So why bring it to me? You don't know me from a can of paint."

"I brought it to you because I know what he did to you, and just like me, you'd love to see him pay."

"So how can I reach you?"

"I wrote my number down on the back of the envelope. I wrote my address as well. I know you'll find me, and I know that the police will come my way, and I want you to know that I'll be waiting."

There wasn't anything left to be said. She got out of the car, closed the door, got in her car, and drove off. Before I pulled off, I looked through the papers one last time. I didn't call Lamar, because I knew he would probably try to talk me out of it. I had to do this.

I took the envelope and drove it down to the police station. I actually found a man outside to take it in for me. I paid the man to take the envelope inside. I never gave my name or anything. After he dropped off the envelope, I returned to my car and left. It wasn't long before it was all over the news. News reports were everywhere, saying that there was a ruthless drug lord who had been arrested in connection with multiple homicides. It also said that Alisha had been shot but was in stable condition, but another male at the scene had not survived his wounds. I was ecstatic, couldn't have been any happier. I did tell Lamar eventually what I'd done, and he said that I was right—he would've tried to talk me out of it. It felt good sleeping at night knowing that he was put away for life. That is, until right before his execution when a stay was granted.

Chapter Thirty-four

Total Devastation - Flashback

Alisha

After I made it home, I flopped down on the couch and closed my eyes. Tears were still falling as I thought about the conversation I just had with Dontay. Even though Desi left me high and dry, I still loved him. I turned on the television before falling to sleep. It wasn't long before I was awakened by a knock at the door. Once I opened it, I was surprised to see Desi standing before me looking sexier than I'd even seen him.

"Hey, Desi, what brings you here?" I asked while leaning against the door.

"You called my phone and when I tried to call you back I couldn't get through."

"So, you came all the way over here because I didn't answer the phone?"

"No, because niggas in the street are talking, and I was worried."

"What do you mean niggas are talking?"

"Look, let me come in so we can sit and talk," he insisted.

"Sure, come on in," I said as he began to make his way into my apartment. "So who's talking? And about what?"

"About you being involved with these hustlers who are somehow popping up dead. Niggas think you have something to do with it."

"What?" I asked, surprised.

"That's the word on the street. I was just worried since I hadn't seen you in a while. It was kind of weird that you called me."

"I apologize if I worried you."

"So what did you need when you called?"

"I wanted to ask you a question."

"About what?"

"About your feelings for me. I wanted to know if you ever really loved me."

"I have a lot of love for you, Alisha."

"But I mean, did you really love me?"

"I almost married you, Alisha. Of course I really loved you and regardless of the outcome, I still do," he responded, before turning his head to avoid staring me in the eye.

I knew that I had touched a soft spot. It was that answer that made it harder for me to do what Dontay needed me to do. Had he told me he never really loved me, I would've called Dontay and told him to count me in.

I wanted to tell him what Dontay was planning to do, but I knew that he would be furious at me. I needed to feel his touch one last time before he walked out of my life for good. I moved close to him, and looked into his eyes before I began to kiss him. I could feel him trying to pull away, but I wasn't going to allow it.

I slowly unzipped his pants sticking my hand inside to caress his dick. It was then that I realized how much I'd missed him. He began to get into it as he rubbed his hands across my breasts. I wanted to taste him so I got down on my knees putting all of him into my mouth.

Giving head was something that I enjoyed to the fullest since I had mastered my technique while dealing with him. You could hear the sounds of me sucking his dick, as the apartment was quiet as a mouse. I moved up and down as I showed his balls some attention with my free hand.

As he became more excited, he lifted me up and turned me around so that my ass was in his face. He pulled down my shorts before lying back on the sofa, instructing me to sit on his face. I obliged and as he stuck out his tongue. I placed my clit on top of it and moved in circles. I quickly climaxed all over his tongue.

He continued to suck my clit as I rode his face like I was racing for my life. I leaned back so that I could stroke his dick while he took in my juices. I couldn't wait any longer so I moved down to sit on his dick. I moaned as his thickness went inside of me. I ground into him while placing my hands on his chest. He stared at me while taking handfuls of my breasts. I breathed heavily as I picked up more speed. Soon he held on to me tightly and exploded. I lay there on his chest thinking about the future. I needed to tell him what I'd been doing, and I needed to tell him Dontay's plans so that he could protect himself.

After he went into the bathroom and cleaned himself up, he sat back on the sofa next to me. He looked at me, and I could tell that he had something on his mind.

"So why did you really call me?" he asked. "Because I know that it wasn't what you said earlier."

"I called you because I . . ." I froze up.

Once he noticed the fear in my eyes he moved closer to me on the sofa.

"I was helping Dontay and that's something I'll regret for the rest of my life."

"What? You were helping Dontay?"

"Yes. Dontay offered me a chunk of money to help him eliminate his competition."

"So what the fuck does that mean? You killed people?"

"No, I distracted them and got them alone. His goons killed them," I said as I began to cry. "I called because you were next on his list and I told him I couldn't do it. I told him how I felt about you, and he didn't care. I wanted to let you know to watch your back. And tell you how I much I care about you."

"So you were going to help that muthafucker kill me?" he yelled, before standing up from the chair.

"No, Desi, I wasn't. I'm scared as hell since he threatened to kill me if I didn't."

"I don't believe this shit, Alisha. What the fuck were you thinking about, getting involved with some shit like that?"

"I was broke. I had no other choice. You left me!"

"That's a bullshit excuse! You could have gotten a job or something! You can't blame that shit on me. You think you're built for this game, and you're not. This shit is serious!"

His cell phone rang, and he paused to answer it. I sat there quietly as he talked on the phone.

He hung up and immediately began yelling. "You set me up, you fucking bitch!" he screamed.

"What are you talking about?" I responded. I had just told him I wasn't going to go through with it.

"That muthafucker has three niggas on their way up here now! I have to get out of here," he said, trying to get to the door.

"I didn't set you up, Desi. I didn't even know you were coming here. Who told you that? Who was that on the phone?"

He didn't speak another word before removing his gun from the small of his back. I was nervous as I backed into the kitchen. Desi opened the door to peek out and was immediately knocked down. His gun flew out of his hand

and as he crawled to get it, one of the three men grabbed him and the other two began beating him. I cried and begged for them to stop. They continued to assault him. As I begged for them to stop, they ignored me.

A few minutes later, Dontay walked through the door with a smile on his face. I was furious as he sat down on my sofa instructing them to keep the beating going. I was helpless. I realized there wasn't anything I could do to save him. Soon Desi was unresponsive. I tried to get closer to him, but each time I was pulled away. To finish him off, Dontay put four shots in his back. The blood immediately began to spill onto the carpet.

"I told you that you were going to finish what you started!" he said as he laughed. "Here's your cash!" He tossed a bag full of cash toward me.

"Fuck your money, Dontay! And fuck you too!" I replied.

"Fuck me? Bitch, I just gave you enough money so you won't have to beg for that shit anymore. You should be thanking me!" he yelled.

"You just killed the one man I cared about, and I should thank you? You can take your money because I don't want it!" I yelled, before throwing the bag across the room. "You are the one who's going to go down for this! I hope you know that!"

"I'm not going down for a damn thing. I'll kill you first!"

"Go ahead, but you're going to die anyway!"

"What?"

"You want to kill me? Go ahead, but remember this: you fucked me raw on numerous occasions, and you should have known better!"

"So are you trying to say you gave me some shit?" he yelled, before walking closer to me. His eyes were opened wide as I tried to back away.

"Yeah, that's exactly what I'm saying. I have HIV, muthafucker, and when your ass is dying, you'll think of me!"

"What?" he screamed.

"You heard me! You'll die thinking of me!"

I was nervous about what he would do next. I wanted this to be over, and if dying was the only way, I was ready to go. I had done a lot of things in my life, and it was too late to turn back now. I stood up off the floor with a million thoughts running through my head.

I found out that I was HIV positive just months before Desi broke up with me. To say that I was devastated would be a total understatement. I went through a lot of different emotions all of which led to anger and revenge. I sat around depressed for weeks before I finally got up and got my ass back to business. One could never truly understand how a diagnosis of HIV can mentally destroy you if you let it. I even contemplated committing suicide a time or two. I never pushed to get back with him for fear that he would find out. I'd been tested previously so I was sure that Desi wasn't the one who I was infected by. Of course I wasn't positive of that, but I didn't want to tell him for fear of his response. I guessed it was my punishment for being loose. Jumping from bed to bed looking for love gave me much more than I bargained for. I was still addicted to sex, and I made sure that I didn't purposely infect anyone, but condoms did occasionally break and once they did I stepped off.

As for Dontay, I didn't care whether he had it. Over the six-month period, I worked for him I had a lot of different feelings for him be it lust, hate, or disgust. He ruined my life and after that there wouldn't be anything left to live for.

While we stood there staring each other down, I thought about the good times I had with Desi. If only

I could turn back time, and never dial his number, he would still be alive. My heart was broken as I glanced at Desi's lifeless body. I wanted to hug him once more before it was all over for me.

I moved slowly over to his body as Dontay continued to stare. I got on my knees and kneeled down next to him as tears began to pour out. I put my lips close to his skin and kept them there for a few seconds. The blood on the floor began to soak into my pants. Dontay became annoyed.

"Get the fuck up off the floor!" he yelled.

I kissed Desi's cheek one more time before rising from the ground. I was no longer afraid of what would happen. I knew that I needed to be with Desi to tell him how sorry I was. If death was my only option then I was willing to take it. I could tell that Dontay was nervous as he began to pace the floor. I knew that the words I spoke to him a few minutes prior were running through his head. HIV was definitely nothing to play with, so I knew that he would go crazy thinking about it long after I was gone.

"You might as well kill me!" I begged him to get it over with. As he raised his gun and pointed it in my direction, I closed my eyes.

"You did this shit the coward's way. You got me to do your dirty work. If you were such a fucking tough guy you would have done the shit by yourself. For that shit you deserve to die, and I hope you die slow!"

I felt the bullet pierce my chest and the warmness of the blood ran down my shirt. I stumbled a little before falling to the floor. He took one more shot at me before things went totally black.

The things that I should have valued I didn't, and even if Dontay hadn't come into my life, HIV would have gotten me. I was fast to give up the ass for cash, and look where it landed me. I had a new outlook on life once I woke up in the hospital and realized that God had given me another chance. The attitude I had toward my illness prior to being shot was definitely different now.

I cared about my life and was going to make the best of whatever time I had left. We should never be so stuck on money that we step out of character to make someone else rich. Money, cars, and clothes have value but life is priceless. It was over, and it was the price I had to pay for being the right-hand bitch to a conniving man who would have never been there for me. It's too bad I didn't realize it all before it was too late.

Chapter Thirty-five

Bulletproof

Desire

I'd been walking around with a bulletproof vest for months because I feared for my life. Now this was yet another reason to keep me on edge. He was sure to order my murder now that he had thirty more days to live. I was shaking as I made it out of the building. Looking around I didn't see either of the two men who had been in the witness area. I briskly walked to my car and once inside grabbed my cell, which was tucked inside of the armrest. I also retrieved my gun and placed it on my lap. I dialed the only person I knew could provide comfort when my nerves were doing jumping jacks all over my body.

"Hey, I was waiting to hear from you. Is it over?" Lamar asked.

"It didn't happen. They gave him a stay," I replied as calmly as I could.

"You've gotta be fuckin' kidding me!" he yelled. "Tell me this shit isn't true," he said in a muffled tone. I could tell that he was just as nervous as I was.

"I wish I were, Lamar. What are we gonna do? I almost shit my pants when that phone rang. I know he's going to have someone after me," I said as my voice shuddered.

Tears had begun rolling down both of my cheeks and landing on top of the gun in my lap.

"Where are you now?" he asked, keeping his composure.

"In the car still sitting outside of the prison. I'm afraid to go home," I said before wiping the tears off of my cheeks.

"Come to my house. I'll meet you there. Do you have your gun with you?"

"Right on my lap," I said, glancing down at my Glock then back out into the parking lot.

"Okay, see you soon. If you see any funny shit, call me."

"Okay. Lamar, I love you."

"I love you too. Everything is gonna work out I promise you."

"Okay, see you soon."

I looked around the parking lot once more before pulling out. Being a police officer, I was always watching my back even when I was off duty. Being in a relationship with a drug kingpin, or any criminal for that matter, definitely makes you more conscious of your surroundings. I was taught that there was always an enemy lurking just waiting for you to slip. Most nights I slept restlessly, always wondering when the next home invasion would occur. My hands were sweating as I sped up the highway trying to make it to Lamar. I always felt safe when I was with him even though he had just as many if not more enemies than Dontay. He could wrap his arms around me and make all of my fears and insecurities evaporate into thin air. Lamar was special, unlike any man I'd ever known, and I was drawn to him like a magnet.

I'd met Lamar while he was attending the police academy. We were extremely close, but more like sister and brother. We'd only known each other for about six months, but he'd become my friend and confidant. He was fine, but not little boy fine. I mean grown man fine like Idris Elba with his bow-legged sexy ass! I loved chocolate men, and if they had a great body and smelled good, I was like putty in their hands. Unfortunately, he was engaged at the time we met and as happy as you'd expect him to be. Instead of impeding, I lusted for him from a distance.

I learned early on about his relationship to Dontay while chatting with him about my past relationships. You could imagine the shock when he told me. He despised him just as much as I did, if not more. After he and his fiancée separated, I'd hoped that there could be a chance for us. I knew how he felt about it, but I honestly didn't care. He was as close to perfect as one could be. He was caring, passionate, and always went out of his way to make his woman happy. I can admit that I was happy when he didn't get married, since she didn't appreciate him anyway. Just as he'd always been a shoulder for me to cry on, I was there to support him. I wanted to be the friend he needed. At this moment, I needed him to be my savior and ensure me that everything was going to be okay.

I was extremely jumpy on the drive. Every pothole and every unexpected bump made me grip my gun a little tighter. The cold steel against my skin somehow made me feel more secure. I arrived in the driveway of Lamar's Main Line home in just under three hours. I hurried out of the car and rang the bell. Lamar swung open the door shirtless in a pair of lounge pants with a .45 in his right hand. Just like me, he was paranoid.

"Hey, you okay?" he said, reaching out his arms and pulling me into a hug.

I immediately burst into tears. He backed into the foyer and closed the door while still holding on to me tightly. I didn't want him to let go. I knew that the end for both of us would be nearing as long as Dontay was alive.

"What am I gonna do, Lamar? I'm really scared. I thought today would finally end it all and help put the past behind me." I tried to wipe away the tears from my face. Mascara was smeared all over my hands.

"I'm going to take care of it," he said.

"How, Lamar? By running for the rest of your life?" I screamed. I wasn't angry with him, but I was angry that I'd allowed my heart to land me in this situation.

"I'm not running. I never have! I'm far from a bitch nigga, and I'll take out every muthafucker he sends my way. I understand you're upset, but I've never been afraid of him. We might share the same DNA, but I'll take his ass out in a heartbeat if I ever get the chance to," he yelled while pacing the floor.

"Lamar," I yelled trying to get him to focus and calm down. He was rubbing the gun against his head as he continued to walk back and forth. "Lamar!" I yelled again. When he refused to answer me, I walked over and grabbed him.

"I'm thinking, D, I'm thinking," he said, staring into my eyes.

"What about your uncle? Have you called him?" I asked.

I thought that his uncle could help. His uncle had run with his father, Jimmy Black, who was once one of the most feared drug kingpins in the city. Back in the seventies and eighties, his name was synonymous with the Philly drug trade. You couldn't speak about a nigga getting money without mentioning his reign. The one thing that he did almost as well as he ran the streets was run through women. He had more than ten children by just as many women. He only married one of them,

Lamar's mother, Theresa. Lamar was close to most of his siblings, except for Dontay, better known as Don. Their rivalry was always over pure hate. Dontay could never get over his father walking out on them. When I met Lamar, he was pretty mum about his brother. Immediately I was attracted to Lamar, and once I learned they were siblings, I understood why. He had some of the same qualities that Dontay did. Once I told Lamar about my on-again, off-again relationship with Dontay, he pretty much let me know that we could never have a relationship.

The two hated each other even more once Dontay murdered their father in cold blood. Lamar went on a path of revenge that ultimately landed both him and Dontay in prison. Eventually Dontay learned about my relationship with Lamar, and it was one of the hardest things that I ever had to do when Dontay ordered me to cut ties with him. I still loved him, and deep down, I always wanted to be with him. I became an enemy when I assisted in getting Dontay arrested for good. Now, you might ask why I'd do it. The answer to that is simple. I learned that Dontay was behind my brother's death, and there wasn't any ring or marriage license that could keep me there after that. The fact that he hadn't even accepted responsibility only made it easier to walk away. With Lamar by my side, we'd done the unthinkable. We'd not only snitched, but also aided in his arrest and prosecution. I used everything that I knew. I nearly lost my badge in doing so, but I didn't care. He needed to pay for what he'd done. Not only to my family, but every other victim as well.

After ten minutes of silence, Lamar finally stopped pacing and sat down on the sofa. I'd since sat down and watched, waiting on him to tell me what we were going to do next.

"Are you okay?" he asked.

"I am now that I'm here with you," I said with puppy dog eyes. I was honestly a nervous wreck.

"Okay, you're gonna stay here for a few days until I figure things out. I'm going to make some calls in the morning. I'll set up the guest room for you, okay?" he said as he kissed me on the cheek and got up from the sofa.

I watched him walk up the stairs and remained quiet. I needed to trust that he knew what he was doing. After a few minutes, he called me upstairs, where I met him at the guestroom.

"Do I really have to sleep in here? Can I just sleep with you? I'll sleep way on the other side," I said. We'd slept together just two nights prior, and he'd been acting weird ever since.

"I'm right next door," he replied with a forced smile.

"Listen, I know you're not comfortable with what happened the other night, and I'll never bring it up again if that's what you want, but I'm afraid, Lamar. I just need to know that you're by my side or I'll never get any sleep," I pleaded with fear written all across my face. Regardless of how much I wanted him to make love to me I wouldn't push because I needed my friend more.

"All right come on," he agreed.

I followed him into his lavish bedroom. I removed my shoes, pants, and bulletproof vest but kept on my shirt. We climbed into his king-sized sleigh bed and positioned ourselves on opposite ends of the bed. After an hour of tossing and turning, I finally fell asleep. I wasn't sure what we were going to do. I was scared to death thinking that soon both of our lives would be over.

***

We were both blessed when we learned that there was a paperwork error and it was now corrected. His execution was rescheduled. Again, I made it there and sat and watched, this time with Lamar by my side. As the clock counted down, I closed my eyes while I prayed that nothing would stop this. Finally, the machine started pumping the poison into his veins, and shortly thereafter, he took his last breath. I felt the biggest relief at that moment, knowing that I could finally breathe.

ORDER FORM
URBAN BOOKS, LLC
97 N. 18th Street
Wyandanch, NY 11798

Name (please print):_____

Address: _____

City/State: _____

Zip: _____

QTY	TITLES	PRICE

Shipping and handling-add $3.50 for 1st book, then $1.75 for each additional book.
Please send a check payable to:
Urban Books, LLC
Please allow 4–6 weeks for delivery